The Trial of John and Henry Norton

Roland Puccetti

The Trial of
John and Henry Norton

A Novel

 Hutchinson of London

Hutchinson & Co (Publishers) Ltd
3 Fitzroy Square, London W 1

London Melbourne Sydney Auckland
Wellington Johannesburg Cape Town
and agencies throughout the world

First published 1973
© Roland Puccetti 1973

Set in Monotype Bembo
Printed in Great Britain by
Ebenezer Baylis & Son Ltd
The Trinity Press, Worcester, and London and bound by
Wm. Brendon, Tiptree, Essex

ISBN 0 09 117930 0

For Glenda and Joe,
who know.

A man's individuality is his demon.
(Diels, 119)

HERAKLEITOS OF EPHESOS

This self is a unity . . . it regards itself as one,
others treat it as one. It is addressed as one, by
a name to which it answers. The Law and the State
schedule it as one. It and they identify it with a
body which is considered by it and them to belong
to it integrally. In short, unchallenged and
unargued conviction assumes it to be one. The logic
of grammar endorses this by a pronoun in the
singular. All its diversity is merged in oneness.

SIR CHARLES SHERRINGTON
The Integrative Action of the Nervous System, p. xvii

Contents

10 *Contents*

Part 4: The Verdict

Part 1: Case for the Prosecution

1. "Henry did it, not me."

I won't pretend I was anxious to take John Norton's case, but then I didn't really have a choice. The sovereign State of Illinois, like others these days, recognises the accused person's right to appointed counsel, whether he wants it or can afford it or not. Actually, Norton was far from indigent, but since he showed no interest in engaging an attorney himself the court assigned me. So now I faced the task of advising someone who didn't want my advice. And Norton, though he wasn't poor, was certainly needy.

The police report kept turning over in my mind as I waited for them to bring him into the visitor's room. Not that there was much to ponder: I've rarely seen such an open-and-shut charge sheet. Not only was Norton home alone with the victim at the time of her death, but the police, answering neighbours' calls after they heard screams coming from the bedroom, actually set off an alarm system by forcing their way into the house. And Norton was found sitting by her body, blood splattered all over him, the murder weapon nearby. My only question, to myself, was why he did it. Depending on the answer to that, I would do what I could to get a reduced charge.

The door opened and he was ushered in. My surprise

was complete. He didn't look like a man who could kill anything, let alone his wife. I placed him at close to fifty, of medium height, thin, mousey-looking. A man so self-effacing in appearance that you could probably talk to him for half an hour at a cocktail party and not be able to describe him afterwards. A bank teller, or possibly a high school teacher of some subject like geography. If I had to guess his passion I would have said it was bird-watching, or perhaps collecting coins. In fact he was an accountant and his hobby was chess. He eyed me warily as he took a seat facing me. I decided to be blunt.

"Mr. Norton, my name is Harvey Shapman. If you don't want someone else to be your lawyer, you're stuck with me. Frankly, you could do better." Well, at least he could smile. The thin lips parted about one-sixteenth of an inch as he started to talk.

"How old are you, Mr. Shapman?"

"Thirty-one." And then, lest he think I'm some sort of ambulance-chaser, "I work with a law firm that specialises in corporate tax problems. It was our firm's turn to offer legal services, and since I'm the most junior partner they stuck me with your case. I'd like to help you, but I think you should know what you're up against. I have only book knowledge of criminal law. I have little trial experience, and I certainly have never defended anyone in a capital case."

He seemed to find that amusing. He actually chuckled.

"You'll do fine for me, Mr. Shapman. You are suitably unqualified."

"What do you mean? Aren't you interested in defending yourself?"

"No, I'm not." A cigarette he'd been holding in the

fingers of his left hand now worked its way up to his mouth. I took out my lighter. He looked at the cigarette with surprise, snatched it out of his mouth with the other hand and put it into a shirt pocket.

"If you're ready to plead guilty I think I can get the charge reduced to non-reckless manslaughter, Mr. Norton. The prosecutor would probably go along with that to spare the time and expense of a trial. You realise this would mean a much lighter sentence, especially since you have no previous criminal rec . . ."

"Guilty?" He looked angry now. "Why should I plead guilty? Do you think I killed Edith?"

I was taken aback. "You mean you didn't? I thought you weren't interested in defending yourself because . . ."

"Because I don't care what they do with me."

"Why not, if you're innocent?"

"Because I lost Edith, Mr. Shapman, and when you have lost everything there is nothing more to lose." He paused. His left hand was groping in the shirt pocket. It came out with the cigarette, very sneakily. "Kill Edith? Why, Mr. Shapman, I wouldn't have harmed a hair on her head."

I reached for my lighter again. He looked down, saw the cigarette, pulled it out of his fingers with the other hand and thrust it into a side trouser pocket. I dimly wondered why he was trying so hard to give up smoking, now when it didn't matter much any more.

"But if you didn't kill her, who did? The police say there was no one else present at the scene of the crime."

"They're wrong. Henry was there. He killed her. I tried to stop him, but he was too strong for me."

"Henry?" My voice came out so strong it startled him.

"Henry who?" Had the police made some terrible mistake? "John. Mr. Norton. Think carefully before you answer. *Who* is Henry? What does he look like?"

"That's the trouble, Mr. Shapman." I watched his head sag and had to lean forward to catch his words. "You see," he sighed, "when you look at me you are also looking at Henry."

2. "There's your motive."

George Carbonari let his head roll back over the edge of his chair and laughed at the ceiling, as if something in its tarnished expanse were terribly funny. Framed by the tips of his polished shoes, now reclining on his desk-top, was a frosted glass door. The letters on it could be read inversely. They said CHIEF PROSECUTOR FOR COOK COUNTY.

"Henry, eh? Oh, that's rich. I didn't do it. Henry did. But of course I'm Henry too."

"He didn't say he's Henry, Mr. Carbonari. Just that when you look at him you are also looking at Henry."

"There's a difference?" Carbonari stopped laughing, but his belly was still heaving. I noticed that even bent over this way he had no bulge above the belt. The man was past forty but as lean as a cheetah.

"Perhaps. Perhaps a great difference."

"Wait a minute. I think I'm getting the picture. Multiple personality. Dissociation reaction. Sometimes he's John Norton, sometimes Henry. Is that your idea?" There was no smile on Carbonari's face now.

"If the man's sick he should be committed, not prosecuted." That was a mistake. A legal tyro like Harvey Shapman should not lecture George Carbonari. Especially George Carbonari.

"Listen, Sonny."

"My name is Shapman."

"Do you think I would be party to sending a mentally ill person to prison for life? Why should I? If he were really sick he'd be behind bars anyway. What does it matter to me, mental hospital or prison? I just don't intend to see him walk off on an acquittal. Norton has no history of mental disorder."

"It could be recent and temporary."

"Sure. That's all you defence attorneys think of. A guy does some terrible thing, something you or I wouldn't do, so he must have been temporarily insane. Balls. John Norton had a thorough examination by the court-appointed psychiatrist. He's as sane as we are."

"The psychiatrist wasn't in that bedroom with Edith and John Norton the night it happened."

"You weren't either. Nor was the judge and jury. Contrary to what you think, the law presumes a man is sane unless there is evidence to the contrary. You don't have any. If you put up an insanity defence I can tell you now I'll knock it to pieces."

I sighed. "Do you have any suggestions, Mr. Carbonari? I mean, what *can* I do for my client?"

Carbonari smiled. Once he thought you had capitulated he became almost benevolent.

"Get him to plead guilty," he said. "I'll reduce the charge to non-reckless manslaughter and with luck he'll be out on good behaviour in eight years." His hands opened gracefully, the wide shoulders shrugged. He seemed to be saying this is the way life is; let's just live it. A benign cheetah. One that's had its prey and wants to digest it peacefully.

Something within me dug its heels in.

"He won't plead guilty. Besides, I wouldn't let him."

Carbonari took his polished shoe-tips off the desk and sat up. The smile was gone without a trace. "Wouldn't you, now? Why not?"

"Because there's no motive."

"You mean we don't know the motive."

"No. I mean what I said. We know there's no motive. The insurance was on his life, not hers. There was no other woman. His friends say he and Edith were inseparable. They did everything together. The vacation trips, the outings, the parties. The last few months everyone says Edith was happier than ever. How could he turn on her after twenty-three years and kill her so brutally?"

"And you think that will get him off?" Carbonari got to his feet and started pacing up and down in front of me, as if I were on the witness stand. "What law book did you get that out of, Buster?"

"Shapman. Harvey Shapman."

"Who told you the prosecuting attorney has to establish a rational motive, or *any* motive, to prove guilt? Listen, Shapman. All I have to prove is that John Norton killed Edith Norton and had no legally acceptable excuse for doing it. No alibi, no entrapment, no self-defence. That's what the law says, and that's what the judge will instruct the jury on. Since when does my failure to supply a motive establish innocence? Since when does it imply he must have been nuts?"

I was shooting in the dark now, but I didn't see what else I could do. "Still, it doesn't make any sense without a motive, Mr. Prosecutor, and you know it."

He stopped pacing and looked at me with slightly more

respect, as if I were a First Year law student who, in spite of his ignorance, might still hold some promise. I was thinking of the same thing he was, namely that the gap in his case provided by lack of obvious motive was just where an insanity defence could take hold. I decided to go on.

"You can instruct juries all you like, but they think in human terms. They ask themselves, would I turn on my wife, or would my husband turn on me like that, for no reason at all? It's unthinkable, because their own happiness and safety are put in question. *That's* when they decide whether John Norton could have been sane when he killed his wife."

There was a knock on the glass of the door, just two sharp raps. A clerk came in and handed Carbonari a sealed envelope. He tore off the seal and extracted a document of about five pages. I waited while he skimmed through it. On page three he stopped and looked at me. The cheetah-glint was back in his eyes. He walked over and placed the third page in my lap.

"There's your motive," he said. I looked at it with a sinking heart. At the top of the page was typed EDITH JANE NORTON, NÉE BREWSTER. On the bottom I recognised the signature of the Coroner of Cook County, Illinois. In between, about a third of the way down the page, someone had underlined this passage:

> *Laceration of anal orifice and rectum to depth of several inches. Sphincter muscle distended and ruptured. Semen traces present, but no blood. FINDING: Post-mortem forcible sexual assault, in this case sodomy.*

3. Congratulations for the Prosecutor

"Ladies and gentlemen of the jury," began Carbonari's opening statement for the Prosecution. "I feel sorry for you."

Scanning the jurors' faces, I felt much sorrier for John Norton, sitting quietly on my right. There wasn't a well-educated, sophisticated-looking or even possibly tolerant face among the twelve. In part it was my fault. I didn't have Carbonari's talent for finding a reason to excuse potential jurors who looked hostile to my client's interests. But even if I had, it would have done little good. Most people called up for jury service were not the sort who might be sympathetic to someone like John Norton, so my pre-emptive challenges had been used up the very first day. Carbonari spread his out over the next two days while I sat by watching helplessly until he filled the box to his liking. The odds, quite simply, were against us.

"I feel sorry for you," he went on, "because you are going to hear things and see things in the course of this trial which the ordinary, healthy person doesn't dream of in the darkest night of his soul."

I wrote "healthy" on my pad. That might be the key to my opening statement for the Defence. But Carbonari's next words caused me to cross it out.

"Don't misunderstand me, ladies and gentlemen. There was nothing wrong with the accused, either mentally or physically, the night Edith Norton died, and I can prove that."

I looked across Norton at Cindy Adams. In many ways she was the only good card I had played so far. Twenty-three but looking not a day older than nineteen, she was fresh out of Northwestern Law School and eager for trial experience. However it wasn't her forensic talents that led me to engage her as assistant Defence counsel. The fact was she looked so pretty and virginal that her mere presence at our bench was an asset. How could the jury believe the terrible things George Carbonari was about to say about my client as she smiled at him, chatted with him, touched him in a fearless, friendly way? I nodded to her and she put a hand on Norton's arm, smiling reassuringly.

"No, what was unhealthy was a certain appetite he had developed, a taste for carnal gratification, a moral degradation, if you will, that he could have suppressed if he wanted but chose instead to indulge at the expense of his loving wife." The jurors leaned forward, incredulity spreading across their faces.

"I shall prove," announced Carbonari, "that the defendant over a period of several months gave indications to others that he had become sexually obsessed."

Months? I wrote this on my pad with a shaky hand. Carbonari must have turned up an important Prosecution witness, and I didn't have a clue who this was. I'd have to ask him today.

"But it was not a normal lust. It was of such a despicable character that I am sure you would never discuss it with your children, even if they now have children of their own."

I looked again at Norton. His jaw was trembling slightly, but otherwise he seemed unmoved. Carbonari's voice raised still another notch.

"It was a lust to have intercourse with a woman in a way forbidden by custom and law. By the laws of this State. By the laws of most countries. By the laws of ancient civilisation. By Biblical law. And, some would want to say, by Natural law itself."

Cindy reached around behind Norton and passed me a note. It read, "Pathans? Arabs? Greeks, i.e. Spartans?" I nodded but put her note into my folder. The jury did not consist of Pathans or Spartans. It consisted of middle-class Christian Americans, all born in the Twentieth Century A.D.

"I am going to prove, ladies and gentlemen, that the accused knew this but was determined to have his way at any cost. I am going to prove that on the night of October twelfth he forced his wife to submit to this indignity. But she could not stand the pain. She screamed again and again." Women jurors sat up stiffly in their seats, their faces white.

Cindy passed me another note. It said, "Some girls, I've heard, like it that way. The nerve endings . . ." But I didn't read the rest of her note. It was absurdly beside the point Carbonari was now going to make.

"So what did the defendant do? Did he take mercy on her and spare her? No. Instead he seized a heavy object and struck her with it repeatedly about the face and head. He killed Edith Norton. That is *murder*!"

Out of the corner of my eye I noticed John Norton

trembling much more than before. No, he was not trembling. His face was moving up and down, slowly but unmistakably. He was *agreeing* with the Prosecutor. Carbonari, too, seemed to notice it. He turned towards my client and began advancing on him stealthily, his voice gaining in volume.

"And *then* what did he do? Ladies and gentlemen you will not believe this, but I can prove it to you. He then entered Edith Norton's body when she was already dead. He violated her person, though she was now a corpse. That is *necrophilia!*"

Carbonari was now only five feet from the defence bench. He continued his advance, fixing my client firmly in the eye and raising his voice even more. I began to get nervous. Norton's right hand was tightly clasped, the knuckles showing white through the skin. To my amazement the fingers of the left hand drummed lightly on the bench, as if he were bored or nonchalant. I didn't see how he could do that. But his head continued to move up and down slowly, in rhythm with the prosecutor's words.

"But *how* did he rape Edith Norton? This, ladies and gentlemen, is what I have been saying I shall prove, but which when I state it now you will find too incredible, too disgustingly improbable, to believe. John Norton penetrated her defenceless buttocks, her rectum. In doing so he tore her poor body, which mercifully could feel no more pain. That is how he slaked his lust on Edith Norton, ladies and gentlemen. And that is *sodomy!*"

Carbonari's hand was extended now, a long index finger pointed squarely between my client's eyes. "Those are his crimes. I will prove them."

It happened too fast for me to stop it. John Norton was on his feet and clasping the Prosecutor's extended, accusatory hand in his own, pumping it up and down. He was congratulating Carbonari.

"Mr. Shapman? Defence Counsel?" It was the Honourable Judge Arthur Deakin's voice I heard. "Would you care to make a statement for the Defence now?" I got to my feet.

"If it pleases the court, your Honour, Defence would like to forego a statement at this time. We prefer to reserve this for summation."

Judge Deakin nodded sagely. I would have been a fool to try to explain to that jury why my client was innocent in spite of his agreeing with the Prosecution's charges against him. But in fact I was less worried now than before. In John Norton himself I had the best possible witness for an insanity defence.

4. Bruises on the left wrist

"Call Sergeant Joseph Devereux to the stand."

The first Prosecution witness. Carbonari approached in a relaxed, comfortable way, which is of course the way he felt.

"Your name?"

"Joseph Devereux."

"What is your occupation?"

"Sergeant, Third Precinct, Chicago Police."

"How long have you served with the police?"

"Fifteen years."

"And in that period have you had much experience with violent deaths?"

"Yes."

"Would you tell the court what you were doing the night of October twelfth?"

"Patrolling in the Evanston area with Officers Swenson and Shapiro. It was a radio patrol."

"Did you not get a call to go to 1224 Storemont Avenue that evening?"

"Yes, about 11.15 p.m. The Sergeant in charge said screams had been heard coming from the upstairs bedroom at that address. Next door neighbours had phoned in."

"Did the Sergeant in charge say how long those screams had gone on?"

"*Objection*, your Honour," I said. "Hearsay."

"*Sustained*. Witness will not answer that question."

"Did you have any reason, Sergeant Devereux, to think the call was an urgent one?"

"*Objection*. Same grounds." Carbonari looked pained.

"Your Honour, I am not asking the witness if the Sergeant in charge said the neighbours had reported hearing screams from the defendant's bedroom for twenty minutes or more. I am merely . . ."

"*Objection*."

"*Sustained*. Jury will disregard the Prosecuting attorney's last remarks. There has been no evidence introduced to support them."

"I am merely trying to ascertain why the witness and his fellow law-enforcers did in fact go to 1224 Storemont Avenue."

"Your Honour." I didn't bother to get to my feet. "Defence concedes that Sergeant Devereux and his patrol were ordered to go to the address because of screams reported by neighbours. What we resent is Prosecution's attempt to introduce hearsay testimony with regard to the duration of the screams."

"Continue, Mr. Prosecutor," said the judge. "If you want to introduce testimony regarding the duration of the screams, you may present the neighbours' testimony later on."

"Thank you, your Honour. I may do that. Now, Sergeant Devereux. What happened when you arrived at 1224 Storemont Avenue?"

"The house was dark. We couldn't see from the front

that the upstairs bedroom in the back was lighted." I thought of asking how he could *know* it was, but let that pass. There were bigger problems to come.

"So what did you do?"

"We rang the bell. Knocked on the door. We waited several minutes. Nothing happened. No lights came on. We could hear no noise."

"And how long had you spent before getting to 1224 Storemont Avenue? Since getting the radio call reporting prolonged screams?" He never gave up.

"*Objection.*"

"I mean the radio call reporting screams."

"About twelve minutes. We arrived at 11.30, maybe a bit less."

"Go on. Having knocked on the door and rung the bell, with no response, what did you do?"

"We forced the door. Hit the lock plate with a fire axe."

"What happened then?"

"A burglar alarm sounded. We disconnected this and turned on the downstairs lights before going upstairs to investigate."

"Was it a good alarm system?"

"*Objection.* How could the witness know that?"

The judge looked at me severely. "Let us see what his answer is before we decide."

"I repeat," said Carbonari, "was it a good alarm system?"

"Yes. Burroughs Special System. Costs a couple of thousand dollars to install. We checked it out later that night. You couldn't open an outside window or door without tripping it off."

I withdrew my objection and Judge Deakin nodded. He appreciated young counsel who did not fight time-wasting actions.

"So you went upstairs. What did you find?"

"There was only one door with a light showing under it. We opened . . ."

"*Objection.* Before the witness talked about having to force the main entrance door to the house, setting off alarms and so on. Now he just says he and the other police officers opened this bedroom door. Jury will want to know if that had to be forced or not."

"*Sustained.* Did you have to force the bedroom door, Sergeant Devereux?"

"No, your Honour. It wasn't locked."

"Go on, Sergeant," said Carbonari. "What did you and the other officers find?"

"We found the defendant sitting in an easy chair facing the bed. He had on a silk bathrobe which was partly open. We could see he was wearing nothing underneath. The robe was light-coloured, sort of yellow, and there were blood spots all over it. On the floor beside him was a heavy stone paperweight, marble or something like that. This was covered with blood. His hand and arm too."

Carbonari walked over to the exhibit table and came back with a black stone in his hand. It had red and white streaks in it. I guessed it was onyx. He lifted it up, let it fall once or twice, to show how heavy it was.

"Is this the stone, Sergeant?"

"Yes."

"Your Honour, Prosecution asks that this be labelled People's Exhibit A." In handing it to the bailiff Carbonari

let it slip from his fingers. It crashed heavily to the floor.
I noticed a shiver go through the jury box.

"Now, Sergeant. What else did you find?"

"Well, on the bed there was this lady. I'd say she was
forty-five or -six, but it was hard to tell."

"Why was it hard to tell?"

"Because her face and especially the forehead was
bashed in. Must have been hit a dozen times with that
paperweight."

"*Objection*, your Honour."

"Yes, witness will confine himself to what he saw and
let the jury draw inferences."

"What was the victim wearing, Sergeant? Was she
nude?"

"No, she had on a nightgown. Black with lots of lace,
but it was up around her shoulders. Her body was
exposed."

"Go on. How was she lying on the bed?"

"*Objection.* Witness did not say she was lying on the
bed. He said there was a lady on the bed."

"Well, your Honour, what does my young colleague
here think she was doing on the bed? Sitting up? Standing?" Titters ran through the courtroom.

"Perhaps you could rephrase your question, Mr.
Prosecutor."

"Very well. Was this woman lying down on the bed?"

"Yes, sir."

"And in what position?"

"On her side, one leg crossed over the other, her arms
hanging over the side, her face buried in the pillows."

"But before you said her face was bashed in. How
could you see it if she had it buried in the pillows?"

"That was after we turned her over. At first we couldn't see her face, though from the amount of blood on the pillows we expected to find it cut up or beaten."

"I see. Now am I right that if one leg was crossed over the other and her nightgown was up the buttocks were exposed?"

"Yes. They sure were. In fact . . ."

"In fact what? Speak up."

"Well, there was a pillow under her hip too."

"You mean the buttocks had been deliberately raised?"

"*Objection*, your Honour. He's asking the witness to make inferences again."

"I'll restate that question, your Honour. You mean the buttocks were in a raised position?"

"Yes."

"Because a pillow had been placed . . ."

"*Objection.*"

"Because there was a pillow between the victim's hip and the bed?"

"That's right."

"So that it looked to you as if her body had been positioned that way in order . . ."

"*Objection*, your Honour. He's leading the witness."

"Your Honour, I am asking the witness what went through his mind as he contemplated this poor woman's body. If he suspected sexual assault. Sergeant Devereux is a man of experience. When he sees a woman in this position . . ."

"No one is doubting Sergeant Devereux's experience of the positions of love, your Honour. But what he suspected is not admissible evidence."

"I think I'll have to go along with Defence on this, Mr. Carbonari. Objection *sustained*."

"All right. Were there any marks on the exposed parts of the victim's body, Sergeant?"

"No."

"None whatever? No scratches or bruises?"

"Not that I could see. Of course she went for autopsy afterwards and . . ." I didn't have to object. Carbonari cut him off with a wave of the hand and turned away.

"That's all. Thank you, Sergeant. Your witness, Mr. Shapman."

I stood up quickly and gave Cindy a weary look before crossing to the witness box.

"Sergeant Devereux, you testified that when you and Officers Shapiro and Swenson arrived at the bedroom door you found it unlocked. You were able to walk right in. Is that correct?"

"Correct." I could tell he was being hostile, probably because of the gratuitous remark I'd made about his sex life. I'd have a hard time getting anything out of him.

"So there was no attempt on the defendant's part to keep you out?"

"No, as I said, he was just sitting there looking at her."

"Even though you had set off an alarm system minutes before, breaking into the house with a fire axe."

"Yes."

"Now you have said a lot about Mrs. Norton's body but little about Mr. Norton himself. While you were examining her he said nothing to you?"

"No, and we didn't question him, either. You know, these days if a suspect doesn't have a lawyer right there you can't . . ."

"Just answer my questions, Sergeant. He said nothing *to you*. Did he say anything at all?"

"Just mumbling."

"Mumbling? What was he mumbling?"

"I couldn't hear him so good. But it sounded like, 'Poor Edith'."

"'Poor Edith'? He said, 'Poor Edith'?"

"Yeah, over and over again. 'Poor Edith'."

"He didn't say anything else?" With luck he'd repeat it again.

"No, just 'Poor Edith'."

"I see. Now you testified that Mrs. Norton had no visible marks on her body, no signs of having been assaulted."

"*Objection*, your Honour." Carbonari was on his feet before I could turn to see him. "I wasn't allowed to ask if the witness thought she may have been assaulted, now counsel wants to ask if witness thinks she had *not* been assaulted."

"*Sustained*. Re-phrasing is in order, Mr. Shapman."

"Very well. There were no marks on her indicating assault?"

"No."

"Now how about the defendant? Did he have any scratches or bruises on his person?"

"Yes, he did."

"He did?" I had really walked into that. I could hear Carbonari chuckling behind me. "Where?"

"There were deep bruises forming around his left wrist."

"Only there? You examined him all over?"

"Well, not exactly. But like I said he had nothing on

2

under the robe and when we asked him to dress I got a good look at him."

I was lost now, but could see no other way to go. If I didn't, Carbonari would pursue it on Re-direct anyway.

"What did you think made these bruises?" Not at all to my surprise, Carbonari did not object.

"Fingers closing around the wrist. I could see individual finger-marks forming there. You know, yellowish-grey at first, but deep blue later on. The thumb-print was especially clear."

"Thank you, Sergeant." I walked away, cursing under my breath.

"Just a minute, Sergeant. I have one or two more questions." Carbonari smelled blood all right. "You said the thumb-print was especially clear. I'd like to know what position it was in relation to the finger-marks. Was it like this?" He seized Devereux's left wrist with his right hand and raised it above his head.

"Yes. Like that." One could see the paperweight in that hand, descending on Edith Norton's head.

"It could have been made by a frantically frightened woman trying to defend herself from a blow in the face or on the head?"

"Yes, if she was very strong. Or scared enough. They say . . ."

"Would that account for the position of the marks on the accused's wrist as you observed them that terrible night?"

"Yeah, and that's what puzzled me." Carbonari let go of the wrist.

"Puzzled you? What puzzled you?"

Was it possible Carbonari had gone too far as well?

He stepped back and dropped his hand, waiting for an answer.

"She couldn't have made the marks. You see, she had no right hand."

Only then, fool that I was, did I remember the Coroner's report. The opening sentence said: "White, well-nourished female of approximately forty-three years, normal except for missing right forelimb: stump indicates old surgery, probably accidental loss in childhood."

"Sergeant Devereux. You and the other two officers examined the Norton home carefully?" He was almost frantic now. "You dusted it for fingerprints and footprints?"

"Yes, we did."

"Did you find evidence that any third person had been in the house on October twelfth, that evening?"

"Absolutely none."

"Thank you, Sergeant. You may step down now."

5. "But Edith *was* raped."

"Doctor James Fahy, please. Will Doctor Fahy take the stand?"

He was portly and almost jolly-looking. The nose shone suspiciously red, the fingers trembled. I wondered if Carbonari, who was standing close to him, could smell liquor on his breath.

"Doctor Fahy, would you please state your qualifications?"

"I have an M.D. degree from Cleveland Reserve University and did my internship in pathology at Cook County Hospital. I have been chief pathologist in the Coroner's office for the past nine years."

"Did you write the report on Edith Norton here?" Carbonari waved a copy of the document. He seemed well-recovered from this morning's disaster.

"Yes, I did."

"Your Honour, let this be Exhibit B for the People. Now, Doctor Fahy, was it as a result of doing an autopsy on the remains of Mrs. Norton that you wrote this report?"

"It was."

"What did you find to be the cause of death?"

"Multiple depressed fractures in the region of face and forehead, causing severe brain damage."

"Was there much blood about the head and shoulders of the victim when she was brought to you?"

"Yes, as one would expect from such gross injuries."

"In other words, she was alive when those injuries were received?"

"Of course."

"Would there have been much blood had she been dead before receiving them?"

I could see where Carbonari was going, but not how to stop him.

"*Objection*, your Honour. The question is hypothetical and not factual."

"I think I'll let that one go by, Mr. Shapman. Dr. Fahy has ample experience in his line of work to answer it. Objection *overruled*."

"No, there would not, since the heart would have stopped pumping. Unless she were hanging face down."

"Thank you. Now Sergeant Devereux testified this morning that he found no marks on Mrs. Norton's body, no scratches or bruises. Did you?"

"No, not on the surface of the body, assuming you mean other than the head region."

"Yes, I do. You say none on the *surface* of the body. Did you find marks elsewhere?"

"Yes, I did."

"Will you explain to the jury where these were and what they indicate to you?"

"The rectal canal was enlarged, stretched, and torn in several places. The opening, or anus, had been ruptured. Semen strains were found beginning at a depth of five inches."

"And what would you say caused these insults to the victim's body?"

"Forcible insertion of the male penis in an erect state, unquestionably."

"Were there blood traces about the anus, which could have been seen on the surface of the buttocks?"

"No, none."

"Isn't that unusual? You spoke of several lacerations."

"Not if she was dead when they were sustained."

"In other words, it is your opinion that the deceased was a corpse at the time forcible entry occurred?"

"Yes."

"Thank you, Doctor. Your witness."

I was going to say "No questions" and let him go, but then I couldn't think of anything *worse* he could say under questioning, so I got up and approached him. A little fishing never hurts.

"Doctor Fahy, at what time did you perform this autopsy on Edith Norton?"

"Well, it was quite late when I got the call. I'd say between one and two in the morning." The bourbon fumes were overpowering.

"Got you out of bed, did they?"

"Not exactly. I happened to stay up late that evening."

"You mean you weren't home in bed? Not even after midnight?"

"No, I wasn't." He looked defensive now.

"Well, were you working in the lab late? Is that it?"

"*Objection*, your Honour. I don't see where this line of questioning is going." Carbonari saw where it was going well enough, and he didn't like it.

"I think we'll give him a chance to show its relevance, Prosecutor. Objection *overruled*."

"Where were you at the time you received the call to do this autopsy, Doctor?"

"I was down the street having a drink with some other employees of the Coroner's office."

"Until after midnight?"

"I'm a bachelor, Mr., er Mr. . . ."

"Shapman."

". . . I don't have a family to go home to."

"Does that mean you spend every evening in a bar?"

"*Objection*."

The judge looked annoyed but interested. "I think I'll hold back on this one too, Mr. Carbonari. Continue."

"Well, I have to be on hand in case of a call, and this is nearby . . ."

"So you do spend most evenings there?"

"Yes . . ."

"Louder, please."

"Yes, I do."

"Doctor Fahy, is there some illness or accident which could cause the kind of distension you observed in the deceased's alimentary canal?"

"You mean a fistula?"

This was a gift which I accepted.

"Yes, a fistula."

"But then there would have been scar tissue. And no semen traces."

"Are you sure it was semen, Doctor?"

"It was a milky white fluid all right."

"You mean you didn't examine it under the micro-scope?"

"No. I didn't see any reason to."

"Couldn't it have been a suppuration of some sort? A discharge due to an infection deeper in the rectum?"

"Well, I suppose that's possible."

It was time to swing wide.

"Doctor, how many papers have you published in medical journals?"

"*Objection.*"

"*Overruled.* An expert witness's qualifications are always fair game, Prosecutor."

"Thank you, your Honour. Answer the question, please."

"I don't go around trying to write up every strange case I encounter, Mr. Shapman."

"So you have no publications?"

"No."

"Do you read scholarly journals in your field? To keep up with the literature?"

"Of course I do."

"What was the last article you read in a pathology journal?"

"I don't remember." He hesitated. "It's been some time now. I'm very busy with my work."

"Yes. Your evenings especially?"

"*Objection.*"

"*Sustained.*"

"I withdraw the question. Dr. Fahy, how many drinks did you have the night you performed an autopsy on Edith Norton?"

"*Objection*. The doctor is not here on a charge of drunkenness."

"No, Mr. Carbonari, but I will allow the question. Defence counsel is questioning the expert witness's competence."

"How many drinks?"

"I didn't keep count."

"What do you drink, usually?"

"Bourbon and ginger ale."

"Singles or doubles?"

"I always drink doubles."

"And how many do you drink per hour? Three?"

"No. One. Or maybe two."

"What time did you start that evening?"

"After supper. About seven o'clock."

"The call to perform the autopsy came after midnight?"

"I've already testified to that."

"So you had ten double whiskies when you operated on Mrs. Norton?"

"I suppose so."

"That's twenty fluid ounces. Almost a whole bottle of whisky."

"Yes."

"Yet you expect this jury to believe you could tell the difference between a fistula condition and rape, or seminal traces—which you didn't bother to magnify on a slide— and an infectious discharge?"

"*Objection*."

"Never mind, your Honour. I have no further questions of this witness." I then walked off, trying to look outraged but secretly ashamed I had given the old man such a hard time. He could probably drink two bottles a night and perform a competent autopsy.

John Norton made my happiness complete. As I sat down he tugged on my sleeve and whispered, "But Edith *was* raped. I saw Henry do it."

6. Slamming the double doors

Alfred Temperton, Jr. made a striking contrast to the previous witness. He was immaculately dressed, tall and slim, and had a pencil-thin moustache which moved up and down like a third eyebrow while he pondered a question. He was so poised I found him arrogant, even condescending. And George Carbonari was taking no chances this time. He had already spent three-quarters of an hour proving Temperton the greatest psychiatrist since Sigmund Freud.

"To sum up, Doctor Temperton, you have the M.D. from Johns Hopkins University, the Ph.D. in Psychiatry from Boston University, did your Residency at Elgin State Hospital, which has nine thousand patients, have published two monographs and sixteen papers in diagnostic psychiatry, are consultant to the Veterans' Administration and adjunct professor of Psychiatry at the University of Illinois, Champaign-Urbana campus. Would you tell the jury now what professional associations you belong to and . . ."

I decided to rattle him a bit. "Your Honour," I said while standing up and stretching, "if it will save time the Defence concedes Doctor Temperton is fully qualified and competent, unlike Prosecution's last witness. Perhaps

Mr. Carbonari can bring this adulation to an end and get on with the trial?"

Carbonari smiled and the judge's eyes twinkled. Temperton looked at me as if I were a smelly dog who had wandered into the courtroom from outside.

"Very well," said Carbonari. "You were appointed by the court to examine John Norton?"

"I was."

"For what reason?"

"To ascertain whether he was fit to stand trial or should be committed to a mental hospital. This is standard procedure in the case of any alleged capital crime."

"And you did examine him?"

"Yes, in the morning of October the thirteenth, prior to his arraignment. I also examined him further at your request, Mr. Prosecutor, on the tenth of November."

I was on my feet again. "Your Honour, may the jury have Mr. Carbonari's reasons for the second examination?" I of course knew them, but I wanted to make him look devious in the jury's eyes.

"I shall bring that out a bit later, your Honour."

"Very well. Continue."

"Would you please describe your examination, Doctor."

"I started as usual by checking the subject's orientation. Did he know his name, where he was and the day of the week, the month? Then I made a routine check on his physical condition. Motor coordination, pupil dilation, knee reflex. These were all normal."

"And how would you interpret the results?"

"That he was not suffering from amnesia, brain damage, or drug addiction."

"I see. Go on."

"Then I administered an intelligence test. The Wechsler-Belleview, which is usually considered appropriate for adults."

"What was your purpose in doing that?"

"To see if he was perhaps mentally deficient."

"How did John Norton do on the test?"

"He scored very well. 119, which is almost superior. Average, of course, is 100."

"Did this conclude your examination?"

"Yes. I certified that in my opinion he could stand trial and did not need commitment."

"Now about a month later I asked you to examine the defendant again. Will you tell the court what reason I gave for this request?"

"You said there was some question of a possible dissociation reaction."

"Please explain what that is."

"Well, it is a rare personality disorder in which the subject develops fairly distinct and in some respects conflicting personalities, and alternates between these. It is also called, for this reason, 'multiple personality'."

"Do you have any way of determining whether someone is suffering from this condition?"

"Oh, yes. Of course the patient may behave very differently from time to time, even call himself by different names. That would be an obvious indication. But since that can be faked . . ."

"*Objection.* Is the witness saying defendant was faking?"

"Your Honour!" Carbonari tried to look offended. "Counsel for the Defence is interrupting my direct examination. He'll have a chance on Cross."

"Yes. However your witness's statement was ambiguous. Could you clarify here?"

"Certainly, your Honour. Doctor Temperton, did the accused, John Norton, behave in the way you just described?"

"No. Not at all."

"Thank you. What you meant, then, was that anyone *could* fake having a multiple personality."

"Exactly, so if there were any reason to suspect this condition it could be determined objectively and scientifically whether the subject has it."

"And how did you, then, test this hypothesis with John Norton?"

"I administered two tests. The Minnesota Multiphasic Personality Inventory and the Rorschach."

"And what were the results?"

"Again, perfectly normal. No indication of personality differentiation whatever. A completely consistent personality profile."

"Thank you, Doctor. Now let me ask you my final questions. First, do you have an opinion based upon a reasonable degree of certainty in the science of psychology and upon the facts, history, and your findings in the tests you made upon the defendant, as to whether or not he was suffering from psychosis or mental illness at the time you examined him?"

"I do."

"And what is that opinion?"

"He was not psychotic."

"Do you have an opinion based upon a reasonable degree of certainty in the science of psychology and upon the facts, history, and your findings, as to whether or not

John Norton knew the nature and quality of the act he performed the evening prior to your first examination of him?"

"*Objection*, your Honour. Witness does not know of any act performed by my client the evening before." It was just a delaying action, but I was pretty desperate by now.

"*Sustained*. Re-phrasing, Mr. Prosecutor?"

"Doctor Temperton, if it were the case that defendant had killed and ravaged the corpse of his wife the night prior to your first examination of him, would he in your view have known the nature and quality of his act?"

"He would, certainly."

"Thank you, Doctor. Now for my very last question. Knowing the nature and quality of his act, would the defendant in your opinion have had or not have had the power or the control over his will to prevent himself from committing that act?"

Carbonari was slamming shut the double doors of an insanity defence—the Mc'Naghten Rule and the so-"Irresistible Impulse" Rule were being foreclosed. I felt powerless to stop him.

"In so far as anyone can control his will, yes. He could have."

"Your witness, Mr. Shapman."

I got up from my chair wearily. Now to see what I could do to prise those doors open.

7. The Ambidextrous subject

"Doctor Temperton."

"Yes?" He looked at me as if I were the obvious source of a bad odour.

"Tell us about that intelligence test you administered. You said the defendant did well on that."

"119."

"Yes. But this would be his total score. The test has different parts to it, doesn't it?"

"Ten parts."

"Did Norton score the same in all parts?"

"Of course not." His expression conveyed the idea that anyone who asked such a question would probably fail the test himself. "He did better in some parts than others."

"In which parts did he do poorly?"

"None."

"Well, in which parts did he do less well than others?"

"In the part which tests memory span for digits."

"Would you explain what that involves?"

"Well, you ask the subject to go forward and backward on digits of, say, three. You know, 9, 12, 15, or conversely, 27, 24, 21."

"He did relatively poorly on that?"

"Relatively, yes."

"And what does that indicate?"

"Nothing serious. Just some short-term memory deficit."

"Didn't that strike you as strange?"

"No. Why should it?"

"Doctor Temperton, do you know what John Norton does for a living?"

"At the moment I can't recall." He tried to smile, but the moustache seemed to be holding down his upper lip. "A typical short-term memory deficit, you see."

"Yes. Very funny. Did you *ever* know what he does for a living?"

"It must have been on his bio sheet sent over by the court, so I suppose I did know at the time I examined him."

"For your information, John Norton is an accountant. In fact he's a Certified Public Accountant."

"How interesting."

"Yes, it is interesting. How could a man who earns a living manipulating figures not be able to count forward or backwards by digits of three?"

"I didn't say he couldn't do that. Just that he didn't do it so well as other things."

"What are the things he did so much better on?"

"Oh, picture arrangement and completion, block design, object assembly, those things that involve comprehension of a total situation, differentiation of essential from inessential details, general intellectual functioning, insight into spatial relations."

"The kinds of things that make for a good mechanic, architect, engineer?"

"I suppose so. Yes."

"Did you know John Norton has never made anything in his life? That he needs a repairman to fix the simplest thing in his house? That he can't even drive a car?"

"No, of course not. How could I?"

"I'll ask the questions here, if you don't mind. Now how could you explain the discrepancy in these test results?"

"What discrepancy?"

"You don't think there's anything strange in a Certified Public Accountant being unable to handle figures well, and in a man with little mechanical ability achieving high scores on things like block design and object assembly? Answer yes or no."

"Well, yes. It is a little unusual."

"Nothing more than that? Tell us now about the personality tests you administered. Take the Minnesota test first."

"There are 550 cards asking questions about the subject's appraisal of his own condition, his moral and social attitudes. The answers are then compared to a large number of answers provided by normal people, to see if there is any significant variation."

"Was there any?"

"Nothing important."

"What variations did you find?"

"Well, he showed a little more concern about personal cleanliness and doing the right thing on social occasions. And there was some evidence of hypochondriasis."

"What is that?"

"Undue concern for one's health."

"Anything else unusual?"

"He indicated some doubts about his masculinity."

"You mean doubts about his sexual virility?"

"Yes."

"Now you knew the charges against John Norton, didn't you?"

"Of course I did."

"Does it seem reasonable to you that a man who is supposed to have killed his wife and then assaulted her body sexually would have doubts about his virility?"

"I really don't think I can answer such a hypothetical question."

"Doctor Temperton, you have testified that test results showed John Norton to be perfectly normal. Now I point to a serious and possibly very significant discrepancy and you say this is hypothetical."

"In my opinion," he said, looking uncomfortable as he started to retreat, "in my opinion the total picture was consistent."

"What about the Rorschach Test? How did he do there?"

"He was shown ten ink-blots made at random and asked what they reminded him of: plant, animal, human, etc. And he was asked why he interpreted them the way he did. I found him fairly dull, self-contained, unimaginative. Certainly not revealing conflicting tendencies."

"Doctor Temperton, if a person suffering from that disorder you called multiple personality were in a particular personality phase at the time he took the test, would he not show a consistent personality profile?"

"He might."

"Would he or wouldn't he?"

"Yes, I believe he would."

"So it is possible Norton, when you examined him, was in a certain phase and therefore did not reveal a dissociation reaction. It is possible he really does have a multiple personality?"

"It is possible." The retreat was moving faster now. I began to hope for a rout.

"When you examined him did the defendant behave at all peculiarly in other ways?"

"No. Absolutely not. Unless . . ."

"Unless what?"

"Well, he was odd in being so ambidextrous."

"You mean he could use either hand equally well?"

"Yes. When he took the Wechsler-Belleview, for example, he did some parts with his right hand and some with his left."

"Which did he do with his right hand?" As I asked the question a recollection came to me. Norton had been doodling on a pad during the whole trial. He hadn't once done that with his left hand.

"Arithmetical reasoning, for example. He did all the problems with the pencil in his right hand. But when it came to performance tests, like copying a design in blocks or arranging pictures in a story-telling sequence, he shifted to the other hand."

"You mean those subtests in which he scored so highly, compared to others?"

"Yes."

"Doctor Temperton, you gave it as your opinion that John Norton was not mentally ill at the time he is alleged to have killed his wife. You said you based that opinion on the facts, history and findings in the tests. Now you sit here and tell us a Certified Public Accountant has trouble with digits, a completely un-mechanical man scores highly on mechanical performance, an alleged sex-fiend doubts his own virility, and on top of that we are dealing with a man who uses different parts of his body to take different parts of the same test. Do you still want to stand by your opinion?"

"Yes. Of course."

"Speak up, Doctor. The jury can't hear you."

"Yes. I am of the same opinion as before."

"Doctor, did you ever talk to John Norton?"

"Of course I did." He was getting really angry now. The moustache began twitching. "How do you think I examined him? In sign language?"

"Very funny, but limit your remarks to answers like yes or no, please."

"I'm sorry."

"Did you discuss the death of his wife with John Norton?"

"No, I did not."

"You didn't? You didn't even ask him how he got into trouble with the Law?"

"I examine patients, not the briefs against them."

"You mean you didn't ask him how he felt at the time of his wife's death, or what happened to her after?"

"No."

"Louder, please."

"I said no."

"Yet you are confident he was in good mental health when these terrible things happened to her? Please speak up."

"I said yes."

"Doctor Temperton, you don't much like people, do you?"

"What do you mean?"

"Would you describe yourself as warm and outgoing in your relationships to others?"

"I am a physician. I try to do all I can to help sick people get well."

"But you don't really care for others, do you? You don't have much sympathy for them."

"I . . . I don't know how to answer that."

"Just answer yes or no. Wouldn't you describe yourself as a *cold* man?"

"Well, I . . ."

"Yes or no?"

"Yes."

"Thank you. That will be all." It wasn't much, but it was the best I could do for John Norton.

8. "He couldn't control his hands around me."

"Elizabeth Vernon," the clerk's voice boomed. "Will Mrs. Vernon please take the stand?"

A hush fell over the courtroom. She was strikingly pretty. Not more than five feet three in her high heels, her hair dark brown and newly bobbed, with hazel eyes and a pert little mouth you wanted to kiss. She wore a brown suit, which was tight-fitting to bring out all the rounded surfaces, and a yellow sweater that did little to conceal grapefruit-sized breasts. Black stockings ran up her thighs out of view, but judging by the calves those would be nicely rounded too. A cute, rather large and cuddly doll. The doll swayed its way to the witness box and perched on the chair. George Carbonari stood very close to her as he opened up.

"Mrs. Vernon, do you know the defendant?"

"Yes, I do." The voice was soft but deep. I looked at Cindy Adams and she winked. This was going to be a tough one for us.

"In what capacity?"

"We work together. I'm a stenographer in the Accounting Department of Greerar Brothers. I've been there five years."

"And during that time you've gotten to know John Norton pretty well?"

"Sure. We're a small department."

"How would you describe him?"

"Oh, the quiet type. Didn't talk when it was unnecessary. Very serious and kind of, well, kind of shy. Or reserved, maybe."

"Did you notice any change in his behaviour the last few months he was working with you?"

"Well, as a matter of fact I did."

"How did he change?"

"This is a little embarrassing to me."

"That's quite all right, Mrs. Vernon. Take your time and choose your own words."

"Well, before last summer he was, like I said, terribly quiet. Not only that. He avoided standing near you when talking, as if he were afraid of getting cold germs or something from you."

"And then?"

"Then about the middle of the summer a change came over him. Oh, he still acted shy and all, but I noticed he brushed against me every chance he got. Particularly . . ."

"Yes? Go on."

"Particularly when I was bending over my desk or reaching into the filing cabinet."

A titter could be heard in the courtroom. Judge Deakin frowned.

"You mean he seemed to be deliberately rubbing against you, against your buttocks?"

She blushed. "Yes," she said.

"What did you do about it?"

"Well nothing much at the time. I mean, I know men sometimes do things like that, and it doesn't upset me a lot. But I did mention it to Craig. That's my husband."

"What did your husband say?"

"He said I should tell him to stop, and that if he didn't I should report him to the manager, Mr. Wilson."

"Did you tell him to stop?"

"Yes. One day I was reaching up on a shelf for some reports and he put his hand on me back there. He even squeezed. I mean, it was sort of a pinch." One or two male jurors, I saw out of the corner of my eye, were suddenly pretending to blow their noses. I was smiling too.

"What did you say to him?"

"I said 'if you ever do that again, Mr. Norton, I'm going straight to the manager and ask for a transfer'."

"How did he react to that?"

Cindy passed me a note. It read, "Are you an ass man or a tits man?" I turned it over and wrote, "Neither, or both", and passed it back.

"Well, that was what was so funny. He acted terribly embarrassed but also bewildered, like he didn't know he'd done anything wrong."

"Was that the end of his advances on you?"

"No. We had this office party that fall, just before the Labour Day weekend. We were all in the bar downstairs before going home, celebrating. I was squeezed in at the bar next to John and we were talking."

"What were you talking about?"

"Well, I had pretty well forgotten the pinching business, and I wanted to be friendly so he wouldn't feel too bad. I was asking about his wife."

"You knew Mrs. Norton?"

"Sure. We'd met at the company's Fourth of July

picnic. I liked her a lot—she was gay and fun-loving—and I admired her for that."

"Why?"

"Well, I mean because of her missing hand. It can't be fun to go through life with a stump of an arm like that. Yet she played all the games . . ."

"Yes, I see." Carbonari's turn to blush. That was the second time he'd forgotten Edith Norton had no right hand. "Please continue."

"Well, I could see he was getting pretty drunk, probably because he wasn't used to drinking. And that was funny too. The bartender asked him if he wanted another and he said no, but at the same time he signalled for a fresh round."

I sat up, listening intently. A police officer whispered into Cindy's ear and she left our bench.

"Then what happened?"

"Next thing I remember I felt cold fingers on the back of my thigh."

"You mean his hand was under your skirt?"

"Yes. So I turned to him and I said, 'what are you doing?'"

"How did he answer?"

"He said he wasn't doing anything. In the meantime his fingers worked under my panties and . . . do I have to tell this?"

"Please, Mrs. Vernon. It is very important."

"Well, then the fingers moved towards the centre and between, between . . ."

"Between the buttocks?"

"Yes. And then he shoved them up. It hurt."

"What did you do?"

"I told him in no uncertain terms to remove his hand. I was really angry and upset."

"What was his reaction?"

"*Objection*, your Honour." I did not get to my feet this time. "Prosecution has been asking for exact words all along. Now he accepts a statement like 'I told him in no uncertain terms'. Defence wants to know what words the witness actually used."

Judge Deakin looked inquiringly at Carbonari.

"Your Honour, Mrs. Vernon has kindly agreed to offer testimony of a very embarrassing nature for her. I don't think it matters . . ."

"I think it does matter, your Honour," I said.

"*Sustained*. Witness will give her exact words."

"Do I have to?" The judge nodded. "Well, I guess I said something like 'Get your hand out of my ass, John Norton'."

A generalised guffaw rumbled through the courtroom. Carbonari glared at me.

"Your witness," he snapped.

"Mrs. Vernon," I said while walking up towards her, "did John Norton ever make any verbal advances to you? That is, did he suggest you go out together, meet secretly in a hotel, anything of that sort?"

She looked at me suspiciously.

"No."

"Didn't you find that strange, as well?"

"What do you mean?"

"Well, if he had deliberate designs on your virtue, why didn't he give some hint of that?"

"I don't know. Like I said, he just couldn't seem to control his hands around me."

"His hands?"

"Yes."

"Both of them?"

"I don't get the question."

"With which hand did the defendant make improper advances that afternoon in the bar?"

"It was his left hand. I know because I was standing to his left, squeezed up against him. The right hand was holding his drink, or his cigarette, all the time."

"You said he declined a drink and at the same time signalled for a round. With which hand did he do that?"

"The left one. I remember because when he said no to the bartender he also covered his empty glass with his right hand."

"Do you recall with which hand he fondled your posterior in the office?"

"*Objection.* Unnecessarily harsh language." Carbonari didn't sound as if he meant it.

"Yes," said Judge Deakin. "Could you re-phrase that, Mr. Shapman?"

"With which hand, Mrs. Vernon, did he pinch you or otherwise make advances to you in the office situations you described earlier?"

"I don't remember."

"Now when this last incident you described took place, you said you were squeezed against the accused and his left hand was suddenly felt to be under your dress. Is that correct?"

"Yes."

"It was then the upper part of your left thigh he first touched?"

"Uh-huh."

"And after his fingers went under your panties he must have touched your left buttock?"

"Yeah. Well, the under part of it. Where the fold of flesh is."

"Mrs. Vernon, we have heard a lot about your left buttock here, but I would like to know where your right one was during the bar incident."

"I beg your pardon?"

"I mean you said you were squeezed against the defendant when his free hand explored the left buttock. Doesn't that suggest the right one was pressed up against John Norton?"

"Well, of course it was. There were all these people pressing up against us at the bar."

"When you told Norton to 'get your hand out of my ass', as you put it, did he continue to appear surprised?"

"Yes, he did."

"He did?"

"Yes, I just said so."

"Isn't that amazing? How could he not know what his own hand was doing?"

"I don't know. I thought he was a really cool liar. And that doesn't fit his personality at all."

"No, it doesn't. I agree with you. Could he have been telling the truth?"

"What?"

"I mean in all that press of bodies, could it have been someone *else's* hand under your skirt?"

"*Objection.* Leading the witness."

"*Sustained.*"

"Were you sure John Norton's hand was caressing your buttock?"

"Well, I couldn't see it. But then he did the same sort of thing in the office, when no one else was near."

"So you just inferred . . . that is, you supposed it was his hand."

"Yes, I did."

"You said before the defendant changed a lot the last few months you worked together."

"Yes."

"Would you say he became a different person?"

"Yes."

"But in fact most of the time he wasn't pinching your bottom, was he? Even in those last few months. I mean that in every other respect he remained the same. He didn't, for example, ask you for a date."

"That's true."

"Then perhaps he became a different person only for a few minutes at a time during the period you described?"

"I guess so."

"Thank you. No further questions."

When I got back to our table Cindy was waiting for me. She leaned over between Norton and me and whispered.

"Important telephone call," she said. "A doctor who treated our client recognised him from the newspaper photograph, though Norton used another name when treated by him. He's willing to testify for us."

"Great news," I said. Then I saw Cindy's face was troubled. "What's the matter?"

"Our client," she whispered.

"What about him?"

"He's got his hand up my dress."

Oh my God, I thought. "Can the jury see it?"

"No. But what do I do?"

I leaned across Cindy and spoke to Norton. "John," I said.

"Yes?"

"Your left hand. Would you please move it?"

He looked down and seemed horror-struck. With his right hand he reached over and pulled the forearm away. Cindy sighed, straightened up, and took her seat quite sedately, as if nothing had happened.

"Next witness?" asked Judge Deakin. Carbonari got to his feet very slowly.

"Your Honour," he said, "the Prosecution calls Miss Rosa Paguera to the stand."

9. The Prosecution rests

"Would you state your occupation, Miss Paguera?"

She was close to forty, olive-skinned and dark-haired, but with that kind of lazy sensuality which I found much more attractive than Elizabeth Vernon's.

"I am a prostitute."

"*Objection*, your Honour." I tried to sound indignant, but didn't have my heart in it. "Are you going to accept testimony under oath of a self-confessed criminal, someone who admits to illicit sexual relations for commercial gain?"

"Hmm . . ." The judge looked at Carbonari inquiringly.

"Oh, come on," he said to me. "You knew this at pre-trial." And then, addressing Judge Deakin, "Miss Paguera has no criminal charge pending against her. She's as free to testify as any citizen."

"Yes, but did you make a deal with her? Did you drop charges in exchange for her testimony?" My voice had risen convincingly. The judge stopped me short; he knew the advantages of deals like this for weary trial participants.

"Your objection is *overruled*, Mr. Shapman. Do you wish to take exception, for the record?"

"No, your Honour. I have confidence in your rulings."

"Thank you, Mr. Shapman."

"But I think it's a shame the State has to stoop to . . ." I let my voice trail off while looking pleadingly at the jury.

"That will be enough." Deakin said it harshly, yet I could see an appreciative gleam in his eye. Carbonari glared at me, then turned back to the witness.

"Now, Miss Paguera, would you tell the court how you came to offer your testimony?"

"Well, I was shown this picture by a police officer and asked if I had seen the man before. I said yes, that he had been a customer of mine."

"Is that man in the courtroom now?"

"Yes. That's him over there." I stole a glance at Norton. His head was bowed.

"On the night of September the first, did you meet this man for the first time?"

"Yes. And the last, thank God."

I made my routine gesture.

"*Objection.*"

Deakin nodded his agreement.

"Jury will disregard the sentence after the word 'Yes'."

"What took place that night, Miss Paguera?"

"Well, I saw this man approaching my usual corner."

"Your corner?"

"Yeah. Where I always waited for business. Corner of North and Clark streets. I wore a short fur coat and just underwear underneath. If the mark—I mean the customer—looked all right I'd open my coat to see if he was interested."

"Go on."

"Well, he looked a little drunk and older and, I don't
3

know, kind of helpless, so I thought he'd be an easy mark."

"Customer."

"Yes. So I gave him an eyeful. And sure enough, he turned on."

"What happened then?"

"Oh, I said something like, 'Quickie or all night?' That's ten dollars or twenty-five, you see." Carbonari cleared his throat awkwardly.

"Just go on."

"Well, he shook his head like he meant nothing doing, but then he reached a hand in and felt my hip, still saying not a word."

"So what did you say?"

"I said, 'You want the Special? That will be thirty dollars but no rough stuff.' And he nodded yes."

"Uh, what did you mean by 'the Special'? Please choose your words carefully, Miss Paguera. The jury . . ."

"Sure. I meant some particular thing he might want to do, like having me pee on him or . . ."

"Yes. I understand. And by 'no rough stuff' what did you mean?"

"Well, none of this crap where I have to hit them with whips or get my nipples chewed off. You know . . ."

"That's quite clear . . ." Carbonari was really flustered now, and I was enjoying his discomfiture. But not for long.

"What happened next?"

"I took him to my room and got undressed. I mean I took off my coat and some of the underwear. Usually they like the garter belt and black stockings . . ."

"Just continue, if you will."

"I got on the bed and gestured to him while he undressed."

"How did you gesture to him?"

"Oh, you know. Moved around a lot and caressed myself, smiling all the time."

"You were on your back?"

"Sure. I gyrated a little and stroked myself. I was waiting to see what he was going to ask for the thirty-dollar quickie."

"The Special?"

"Yeah."

"What did he ask?"

"Nothing. I mean, he never said Word One. But as he got into the bed he made a sign for me to turn over."

"On your stomach?"

"Yes. So I did. I got down on all fours, like they say."

"You were willing that he make love to you like that?"

"Sure. Lots of men like to take the woman from behind. I guess they get a kick out of seeing her bottom move while they're doing it. You know."

Carbonari sputtered. He certainly didn't want to seem to know about this sort of thing.

"Just a moment. By intercourse in the position you describe, Miss Paguera, you mean in the vagina?"

"Yeah, of course. That's why I was surprised."

"What did the defendant do that surprised you?"

"Well, I was all spread and bent over, figuring this mark would be finished in about five seconds . . ."

"Please describe what he actually did, Miss Paguera."

"He got it into the wrong place."

"You mean not in the vagina."

"Exactly. In the other place."

"In the rectum?"

"Yeah. I thought he'd just slipped at first and moved my hand back to correct him. But he grabbed his own, his own . . ."

"Penis?"

"His own penis and forced it in anyway."

"What did you do?"

"I shouted—you know, it hurts—and twisted away to my side."

"Then what did he do?"

"He advanced on me and pulled my top leg up, trying to do it again, while I was lying on my side."

"How did you react?"

"I just screamed. I knew there were two other hookers —I mean, prostitutes—in the same building and I thought one of their pimps, their guys, would come down and pull this maniac off me."

"Did that happen?"

"No. When I screamed he raised both hands above my head like he was going to smash me . . ."

"A threatening gesture? To stop you from screaming?"

"No, I think he meant it. His two arms were shaking with strength and I really thought he would bash in my brains . . ."

"Go on."

"But suddenly he took fright, got off the bed, threw on his clothes and ran out of the room. He didn't leave the thirty bucks, either."

"Thank you, Miss Paguera. Your witness."

I smiled at Rosa Paguera. I actually liked her. She was probably the most honest witness we'd had so far in this trial. And she was attractive.

"Miss Paguera."

She smiled back, but warily. "Yes."

"The fact is John Norton, the defendant, never once said a word to you. Is that right?"

"Yeah. I mean, he didn't."

"On the night of September the first he merely nodded in response to your questions?"

"Correct," she snapped.

"So he might have understood by your offer of a 'Special' almost anything that didn't involve, as you called it, 'rough stuff'?"

"Yes."

"Now you said he persisted in trying to have anal intercourse with you after you twisted off to your side."

"Anal?"

"In the rectum."

"He sure did."

"But you screamed. It was then he raised his arms above you, as you said, shaking with strength, as if he were going to strike you . . ."

"Yes."

"Were the hands separated?"

"What do you mean?"

"Did one hand grasp another?"

"No."

"They weren't connected in any way?"

"Well, yes. One hand held the other wrist, like they were forming a club."

"Which hand held the other wrist?"

"I don't remember."

"But you were now lying on your side looking up, weren't you?"

"Yes."

"Then the hand to your left was his right hand."

She thought a minute. "Yes, it was."

"And his right hand was the one that held the left wrist?"

"Yeah. It must have been."

"Thank you. I have no more questions, your Honour."

Judge Deakin peered at Carbonari with eyebrows raised. He spoke softly. "Re-direct?"

"No, your Honour."

"Further witnesses?"

"None, your Honour. The Prosecution rests."

Part 2: Case for the Defence

10. Something is missing

I stood up, waiting for the courtroom whispers to subside, and cleared my throat nervously. "The Defence calls Doctor Nathan Greenspan to the stand."

George Carbonari jerked upright in his seat, his nostrils sniffing the air for signs of danger. There was nothing he feared so much as a surprise witness, especially in a trial like this one, already so full of surprises.

A bald man of about sixty-five, wearing horn-rimmed glasses and a rumpled pin-stripe suit, ambled towards the witness box. I watched while he was sworn in, keeping one eye on Carbonari.

"Doctor Greenspan," I said while approaching him amiably, "are you a physician?"

He smiled. "Thirty-five years last month, my boy." His voice was mellow, soothing to the ear.

"And what is your medical specialty?"

"Nervous diseases."

"Then you are a neuropsychiatrist?"

"Yes. I normally treat organic mental diseases only." He smiled at the jury. "Easier to diagnose, you know, but harder to cure."

"Doctor Greenspan, did you ever have occasion to treat John Norton?"

"*Objection!*" Carbonari had come up behind me

unnoticed, and when he shouted it almost deafened me. I winced and put a finger in my left ear. "Why did this witness not appear at pre-trial interrogation? I've never seen him before. Defence counsel withheld this witness from me deliberately."

"Mr. Shapman?" asked Deakin.

"Your Honour, the witness's next responses will explain that."

"All right. Will you withdraw your objection, Mr. Prosecutor, at least for the moment? Good. Go ahead, Mr. Shapman."

"I repeat. Did you have occasion to treat my client?"

"Yes, but not under that name. He was not referred to me by another physician, and he gave his name as Thomas Gallagher."

"You mean he just walked in off the street, so to speak, asking for medical treatment?"

"Yes."

"Then it was only when you saw his picture in the newspaper that you realised John Norton was your patient, Thomas Gallagher?"

"Correct. I then telephoned to you. Just yesterday. Or rather, to the charming Miss Adams there." He beamed at Cindy. She winked back appreciatively.

"And when did you speak to me for the first time?"

"Only a few minutes ago."

"So I have not discussed your testimony with you?"

"No, you haven't."

"Nor has my assistant counsel, Miss Adams?"

"No."

"So I don't know what you are going to testify here?"

He smiled again. "Not unless you're a mind-reader."
It was clear he didn't believe in mind-readers.

I turned towards Carbonari. "Satisfied, Prosecutor?"

He scowled but moved back to his table without further protest.

"Now Doctor Greenspan, suppose you tell us about your first interview with the defendant. Take your time and leave nothing out."

"Well, he was somewhat disturbed when he came to me. He described the recent onset of states of confusion combined with tremors and a mild rigidity of the limbs."

"Could you be more specific?"

"Yes. He said that over a period of several weeks he had sometimes 'blacked out' and just before or after this temporary loss of consciousness he experienced a stiffening of his arms and legs, and some trembling in them."

"Did he fall down during these episodes?"

"No, they were too brief for that. One or two seconds at most."

"What did you think might be wrong with him?"

"I thought they might be minor convulsions."

"You mean epileptic seizures?"

"Yes."

A buzz ran through the courtroom. I saw one juror whisper to another, who nodded solemnly. Behind me I could hear Carbonari circling the floor like a hungry barracuda.

"Would that be why the defendant came to you using a fake name, because he was afraid he was epileptic?"

"*Objection!*"

I pretended the other ear had gone too.

"Counsel is leading the witness, your Honour. His question calls for conjecture."

"*Sustained*. Witness will not answer that question. Carry on, Mr. Shapman. Mr. Shapman?"

"Sorry, your Honour. I can't hear you any more."

He smiled and raised his voice. "You may continue."

"Yes. Doctor Greenspan, did you find the defendant suffered from epilepsy?"

"No, I did not."

"But you just said . . ."

"I said I suspected epilepsy. So of course I did an electroencephalogram on him . . ."

"A what? Explain that, please."

"Electrodes are attached to the skull. Brainwave patterns are recorded on a graph. When these show certain configurations you know the patient is epileptic. His didn't."

"The results were negative?"

"Yes."

"What did you do then?"

"I gave him the Tactual Performance Test."

"Would you tell us what that is?"

"I'll do better than that, I'll show you. Now if you'll approach me and lean with both hands on the railing here . . . that's it. Now close your eyes."

"This isn't going to hurt, is it?"

"Not a bit. Now when I touch your cheek or your hand, or any combination of these, you say which cheek or hand I touched. Ready? What was that?"

"My left cheek."

"Good. And this?"

"Right hand."

"Now call these out just as fast as I touch you."

"Left hand. Right cheek. Right cheek and right hand. Right cheek and left hand. Left cheek and right hand. Left cheek and left hand."

"Very good."

"I passed?"

"Yes, you are normal."

"Now how did John Norton do on this?"

"He had no trouble reporting the face regions, but in the combination 'right cheek and left hand' he didn't report my touching the left hand."

"And what did this suggest to you?"

"Damage to the right cerebral hemisphere."

I put my fingers into both ears and waited, but Carbonari just stood there, breathing down my neck. After the laughter died down I turned the witness over to him.

"Doctor Greenspan," he began, "you said you thought there might be brain damage on the right side. Why there?"

"Because the right hemisphere gets information from and controls the left side of the body. That's the way we're hooked up."

"But before you said he could feel you touch his left cheek all right, didn't you?"

"Oh, there's bilateral representation for the head region."

"I beg your pardon?"

"I mean you feel both sides of your face in either hemisphere. It's only below the neck and shoulders that the nerves run primarily from one side of the body to the opposite half of the brain."

"Then you were satisfied his brain was damaged on that side? The right side?"

"No, I didn't say that. I said I thought that might be it. But the EEG I mentioned before didn't show it."

"The electroencephalogram did not show brain damage?"

"No, it was normal. Besides, I knew he felt me touching his left hand, though he couldn't say so."

"What? You knew he could feel you touching his left hand all right?"

"Yes. You see, to test this I asked him to nod his head whenever I touched that hand and he performed perfectly."

"Then why couldn't he *say* when you touched it?"

"Aha! That's the point. He couldn't say when I touched it because the information was not getting relayed over to the left hemisphere, where our speech centres are."

"Why not?"

"Something was wrong with the nerves connecting the two halves of the brain."

"What was wrong with them?"

"They were missing."

Carbonari looked ghastly. "Gone?" he asked.

"Yep," chuckled Greenspan, "completely gone."

"But how did you know they were gone?"

"Well, you'll have to ask Doctor Angell about that. As soon as I suspected the truth I sent him over to her for examination."

11. The Rarest of the rare

"Your name is Catherine Angell?"

"It is."

She was probably forty but looked much less, with fine lines about the face from outdoor exposure. I guessed her sport was tennis, possibly horses, but she was not dressed like a sportswoman. If anything her suit was too severe for such striking good looks. Cindy Adams gazed at her in guarded admiration, recognising a rival for male attention when she saw one.

"You are a doctor of medicine?"

"I am."

"And what is your speciality, Doctor Angell?" I was being all peaches and cream with her, because I had high hopes for her testimony. Carbonari sulked at his table, making notes of everything she said.

"I am a neurologist."

"Did you examine the defendant John Norton on April the thirteenth?"

"I did. But as I think Doctor Greenspan told you, we didn't know him by that name."

"Would you please tell the court how you examined him?"

"I took a pneumoencephalogram. This is an X-ray taken after you have drained the ventricles of fluid and replaced it with air by spinal injection. Since air has a different density, the empty spaces stand out clearly in the photographs. If some part of the brain is missing, that would show too."

"And what did these show?"

"Central necrosis of the corpus callosum."

"Could you explain that?"

"The main nerve connections between the two hemispheres of the brain were eaten away."

"Do you have copies of the X-ray photographs with you?"

"I do." She slipped them out of a large manila envelope and handed them to me. I made a great show of looking at them carefully, although as far as I knew they could have been pictures of dried-out sponges. "I have marked with arrows," she added, "the areas where degeneration is most obvious."

"Thank you, Doctor. Your Honour, I should like these marked as Exhibit A for the Defence. Would the Bailiff also pass them around to the jury? Now Doctor Angell, would you tell us what caused these nerve connections to be eaten away like that?"

"Well, it's the rarest of rare brain diseases. What is known as Marchiafava-Bignami Disease."

"How did it get that name?"

"It was discovered and first diagnosed by two Italian physicians at the turn of the century."

"You said it's the rarest of rare diseases. Just how rare is it?"

"A few dozen cases have been reported from Italy, only three in this country before."

I stopped right there, sniffing danger myself. Better to let Carbonari bring out what I thought that implied.

"Doctor Angell, would you say this is a serious disease?"

She smiled. "Certainly."

"How serious?"

"It's usually progressive and fatal."

"Thank you. Your witness, Mr. Prosecutor."

"Doctor, you said only three cases of the illness have been reported in the United States, didn't you?"

"Yes."

"What was their nationality?"

"The first was an Italian living in Boston."

"And the second?"

"A Swiss-American of Italian extraction from Florida."

"And the third? Was he Italian too?"

"No."

Carbonari looked disappointed. "He wasn't?"

"No, he wasn't."

"Well, how do you explain that fifty or so cases were all Italians but not this last one?"

"He had Italian friends."

"I don't understand."

"They supplied him with the wine."

"*What* wine?"

"You see, every case reported was connected with addiction to a crude red wine Italian peasants like to make and drink."

"You mean what is popularly called 'Dago red'?"

"Exactly."

Carbonari turned away and scratched his scalp, exactly at the middle. I thought that was hilarious, since he's of Italian origin, but I suppressed my giggle. He whirled back at Doctor Angell, smiling now.

"Then this rare disease is caused by a special wine addiction?"

"That is the received opinion, yes."

"Was the defendant John Norton addicted to this wine?"

It was her turn to smile. "Definitely not."

"Thank you, Doctor Angell. She's all yours, Mr. Shapman."

I approached her again with great caution and respect. She was a formidable witness, capable of turning the tables on you with just one quick answer.

"Doctor, are you and Doctor Greenspan writing a paper on the case of John Norton, *alias* Thomas Gallagher?"

For once I shocked her. "How did you know?" she asked.

"Oh, I don't know," I said, "but it must be interesting to discover a case of Marchiafava-Bignami Disease without alcoholism as a contributing factor. What other cause was present in the earlier cases?"

"Malnutrition, in every case. More specifically, avitaminosis, lack of vitamin B_1."

"Could that alone cause the disease?"

"It has in starving dogs, but it was never noted in humans before."

"Did John Norton have avitaminosis?"

"He certainly did. For months prior to his tremors he had not eaten properly."

"Why not?"

"A stricture of the oesophagus. A partial closing of the throat."

"Thank you. Your witness again, Mr. Carbonari."

12. Radical disconnection

"Doctor Angell, you said before that this disease is known to be caused by wine addiction." She didn't turn a hair, as I knew she wouldn't.

"I said that was the received opinion."

"By 'received opinion' you mean the overwhelming opinion of your expert colleagues, don't you?" Carbonari looked meaner than usual.

"Yes, but they always recognised malnutrition as a contributory cause too."

"Isn't this because alcoholics usually don't bother to eat properly?"

"Neither do starving dogs, but they are not alcoholics."

The Prosecutor drew back sharply; he wasn't fool enough to get into this kind of argument with Catherine Angell.

"All right," he conceded generously, "let us suppose this very rare brain disease can be caused by avitaminosis alone. Now you said it is a progressive and fatal disease, didn't you?"

"I said it is usually so, yes."

"How long does it take to kill, normally?"

"That depends on the stage at which it is detected."

"Well, when the whole central nerve connections are gone, how long does it take then?"

"A matter of weeks, possibly a couple of months."

"When did you examine the defendant the first time?"

"I told you. April the thirteenth."

"But that's almost a year ago. And you said his corpus callosum or whatever you call it was already completely gone then."

"Yes."

"But he hasn't died."

"That is obvious," she smiled, "since he's sitting here now."

Carbonari was jarred by the ripple of laughter around him. "Then either your description of the disease or your diagnosis of the defendant must be wrong," he said angrily.

"Not at all," she answered. "Since wasn't alcoholic, all we had to do was give him massive doses of vitamin B_1 and have his throat cleared surgically so he would eat properly again."

The Prosecutor suddenly beamed. This is what I meant about Doctor Angell's testimony—you never knew where it would take you next.

"So, Doctor . . . you *cured* the defendant of his disease. Is that what you are saying?"

"We arrested it, yes."

"And when was that, approximately?"

"By mid-May of last year he was able to work normally again."

"Would you say that between the middle of May and mid-October he was no longer in need of medical care?"

"Provided he kept to a good diet, I would expect no further complications. Definitely."

Carbonari looked significantly at the jury, then at me, then back at the witness.

"Did the defendant have any more of these blackouts described by Doctor Greenspan after your treatment of him?"

"Not so far as I know, no."

"So those were due to the disease in its active stage, which you and Doctor Greenspan stopped once and for all?"

"Apparently. Had they recurred he surely would have come back to us for further vitamin injections."

"Then as far as you can tell he was restored to normal health?"

"Yes."

"And without information to the contrary you have no reason to doubt he was perfectly normal in mid-October as well?"

"If you mean with regard to the brain-diseased condition he had before, I would say he was, yes."

"Thank you, Doctor. She's all yours, Mr. Shapman."

This time I was rushing at her, while Carbonari strolled jauntily back to his table.

"Doctor Angell, you say John Norton was perfectly normal after he received these vitamin treatments. You mean his brain was no longer diseased, don't you?"

"Yes."

"But would you say his brain was otherwise normal?"

"What do you mean?"

"Did the nerve connections between the halves of his brain grow back after the disease was arrested?"

She broke into a grin. "Are you serious? Tissue from the Central Nervous System doesn't regenerate."

"Never? It never grows back?"

"It does in toads and salamanders, but not in human beings."

"So then in mid-October, or any time since the disease was arrested, John Norton did not in fact have a normal brain?"

"He hasn't had a corpus callosum, if that's what you mean."

"That is what I mean."

"Well, of course not."

"Now Doctor, tell me this. Is not the human eye a complex organ?"

"The eye? Of course."

"To be able to see what we see there must be a lot of nerve connections between the eye and the brain, isn't that right?"

"Yes."

"How many nerve connections are there?"

"About a million fibres in the optic nerve."

I looked incredulous, turning towards the jury so they could see how astounded I was.

"A *million* fibres?"

"Approximately." She was smiling at my performance.

"Then tell me, Doctor, how many nerve fibres are there in the corpus callosum?"

"Estimates vary. I suppose two hundred million would be a safe guess."

"*Two hundred* million? Two hundred times as many nerve fibres as the optic nerve, the one we see with?"

"Yes."

"Then my client, the defendant, has been walking around with two hundred million nerve fibres missing from the very centre of his brain?"

"How many times do I have to answer the same question?"

"Oh, I'm sorry. But you will agree this is no small, trifling loss to a human brain?"

"Loss of any tissue from the brain is potentially serious."

"Wouldn't you say this is a *drastic* loss?"

"Well, it disconnects the cerebral hemispheres pretty effectively."

"Is that a yes or a no? Isn't this a drastic disconnection of, or interruption of, the person's normal mental life?"

"I would say it is a radical disconnection, anyway."

"Then his mental life after the disease could not have been normal, could it?"

"Not in every respect, no."

"Thank you again, Doctor. Back to you, Mr. Prosecutor."

He didn't look worried at all, which really worried me.

"Doctor Angell, about how many nerve cells are there in the normal human brain?"

"No one knows."

"Take a guess."

"Fourteen thousand million."

"Really? That's enormous. Now tell me, is it not true that people have lost sizeable portions of their brains without mental impairment?"

"Yes. It all depends on where the loss occurred, on age, on . . ."

"So loss of part of the brain does not itself guarantee loss of brain function?"

"Not by itself, no."

"What happens when people lose the corpus callosum?"

"There is some accompanying loss of short-term memory. They have trouble remembering telephone numbers or directions or how a story they are reading began."

"Could they remember their names, who they are, what schools they went to, their loved ones?"

"Yes, there's no loss of long-term memory."

"What else? What other changes would you expect?"

"None. That's really the funny thing about the corpus callosum. Because it's such a rich fibre tract, you would expect its loss to be terribly handicapping. But it isn't. Some people are born without it and we don't discover that until autopsy."

"Would it be safe to say, then, that to the best of your knowledge the disease, once it was arrested, did not leave behind organic damage involving continuing mental impairment?"

"Provided there was no damage to the rest of the brain, yes."

"Was there to your knowledge any other brain damage?"

"No, there was not."

"Mr. Shapman?" He smiled as if he were letting me have the next dance, a slow number he didn't care for anyway. As I approached the witness box wearily a simile came to me: I was for ever knitting a defence and George Carbonari was for ever unravelling it.

"You said a moment ago, Doctor Angell, that you wouldn't expect any changes other than loss of short-term memory in John Norton."

"I did."

"What about personality changes?"

"No, I wouldn't expect that."

"You observed none in the defendant?"

"None."

"How well did you get to know him?"

"I talked to him several times."

"Before or after the successful treatment?"

"Once before. Three or four times afterwards."

"That's all?"

"Yes."

"Then how can you be sure his personality didn't change?"

"I didn't say it hadn't. I said I observed no changes."

"So there could have been a change between mid-May and mid-October without you knowing it?"

"It's possible, I suppose."

"Your answer is 'Yes, there could have been a change'?"

"Yes."

"Thank you."

I felt like a poker player who's drawn his last card and hasn't improved. If Carbonari didn't give something away in the next questions I wouldn't have bet much on the hand I held.

13. A Little peculiarity

"Doctor Angell, I know you're very busy and I won't keep you long." Carbonari was exuding confidence now. He was going to sew it up, or so he thought.

"That's all right." She took in his good looks again, smiled, unconsciously brushed her hair into place. "I'm glad to be of help."

"Thank you, Doctor. Now Doctor, if it came to your attention that a patient who had recovered from this disease after treatment, though no longer having a corpus callosum, subsequently developed a sexual perversion, would you think that might be due to the brain loss itself?"

"Not at all."

"Why not?"

"I don't see any reason for it. Whatever drives a person is presumably in the deeper brain structures, and it is not affected by loss of the connecting nerves between the half-brains. As I said, the disease takes out only those connections."

"That wouldn't affect sexual orientation?"

"I don't see how. Of course drives can be deflected by what develops in the cerebral cortex, but even there the surgery doesn't have any effect."

"Please explain why."

"Because separation of the hemispheres doesn't *add* to what's already there. It's like disconnecting Siamese twins. You don't change either twin by freeing them from each other. Of course the difference here is that Siamese twins have two bodies to begin with, while the hemispheres control the same body."

I sat up and began jotting notes on my pad. But I had to listen to Carbonari at the same time.

"So it is your opinion that separation of the defendant's brain hemispheres could not have prevented him from knowing the nature and quality of any act he subsequently performed?"

"Certainly not."

"Could it prevent him from having the power or control over his will to avoid committing that act?"

"Again, no. Definitely not."

"Thank you very much. I hope my learned junior colleague here will let you get back to your busy schedule without delay."

I shuffled my notes and took them up to the witness box with me. She waited expectantly.

"Doctor Angell," I began, "your testimony so far gives me the impression that the sole purpose of the two hundred million nerve fibres gone from John Norton's brain was to help him remember telephone numbers and how stories began. But Doctor Greenspan in his testimony said that as a result of the disease the defendant couldn't say with eyes closed when his left hand was touched. Do you agree that was the case?"

"Of course the commissural connections relay information from one hemisphere to the other. That's their primary function."

"You mean each hemisphere originally gets information the other doesn't get?"

"Yes. For example, what you see to the right of me goes into your left hemisphere, and what is to the left is seen by your right hemisphere. The nerves cross over that way."

"And then what I see to the left of you is relayed through the corpus callosum from my right hemisphere so I see it also in the left one?"

"Yes, and vice-versa."

"So if you remove my callosum I can't relay that information any more?"

"Correct. But of course it doesn't make much difference."

"Why not?"

"Well, when you're looking in my direction rapid eye movements scan objects in the whole visual field, so each hemisphere gets pretty much the same information independently. It's only if you fix your eyes on a particular point that there's a difference."

"What difference?"

"Suppose you look directly into my eyes."

"Yes?" They were a beautiful clear grey colour.

"If what you see to each side of me were flashed very quickly at you, too fast for your eye movements to take it in, half of what you see would be seen by one hemisphere, half by the other."

"I'm following."

"Now without the commissural connections you wouldn't be able to say what's to the left of me."

"Why not?"

"Because that was seen by the right hemisphere only,

which has no speech centres. These exist only in the left hemisphere, and the information was not relayed to it."

"You mean I wouldn't be able to say I saw Judge Deakin there, though I did see him with my right hemisphere?"

"That's right." She beamed at me like a bright pupil.

I could hear Carbonari making impatient noises. I dared not slow down now.

"What about hearing sounds?"

"No, that wouldn't be different. Each hemisphere would hear pretty much the same sounds independently. You see . . ."

Carbonari was on his feet again. "Your Honour, this is all very interesting scientifically, but I wonder . . ."

"Yes . . . Mr. Shapman, can you see me all right?"

"With both hemispheres, your Honour."

"Good." He chuckled. "Are you going somewhere here?"

"I think so, your Honour."

"All right, but we'll need a link-up soon."

"Thank you. Doctor Angell, what about feeling things? Say an object I'm holding in one hand."

"The opposite hemisphere would know what it is, but if you couldn't see it the hemisphere on the same side could only guess."

"Really? Then if I hold my hands behind my back like this and someone places an object in my left hand—say a key—I wouldn't be able to say what I'm holding there?"

"That's correct. However if I named a series of objects —comb, pipe, fountain pen, key—you might nod your head affirmatively when I said 'key'."

"The way the defendant was able to indicate by

nodding that Doctor Greenspan had touched his left hand?"

"Yes."

"Doctor Angell, could my left hand pick up an object behind me, or to my left side, while I am looking straight ahead at you, without my speech hemisphere knowing it?"

"There is a little peculiarity about that."

"What peculiarity?"

"Sometimes the right hand doesn't know what the left is doing."

14. You do sometimes get these conflicts

"*Objection:* Your Honour, this has gone far enough. He's obviously stalling . . ."

"Just a moment, Prosecutor. Mr. Shapman, you'll have to make all this relevant and material."

"Yes, your Honour. I intend to. If you'll just bear with me a little longer . . ."

"Very well. But do get on with it."

"Thank you. Doctor Angell, are you familiar with the Wechsler-Belleview Intelligence Scale?"

"Yes."

"Would it surprise you that a Certified Public Accountant who had this disease did poorly on counting backwards and forwards in digits of three?"

"No. As I said, there is some loss of short-term memory."

"Would you be surprised if he had been very unmechanical before the operation but scored highly on performance tests like block design, object assembly, picture arrangement?"

"With which hand?"

"Using the left hand, though he is normally right-handed."

"No, I wouldn't be surprised. The right hemisphere, controlling the left hand, is much better at geometrical problems, relative sizes of things, and recognising shapes. It would probably take over on the performance part of the tests."

"Are you also familiar with the Minnesota Multiphasic Personality Inventory?"

"I am."

"And with the Rorschach test?"

"Yes."

"Would it surprise you that these tests failed to reveal any personality deviance when administered to a person whose hemispheres are disconnected?"

"Not at all. If there were any personality differences between the hemispheres those tests wouldn't show it."

"Why not?"

"Because they are administered verbally. Only the left hemisphere would be supplying answers."

"You mean the right hemisphere, if it could talk, might supply different answers?"

"It might. I don't know."

"Thank you. Now Doctor Angell, you said before that sometimes one hand doesn't know what the other is doing."

"Of course I meant one hemisphere might not know what the same-sided hand is up to."

"If you were squeezed up against me in a bar, say on my left side here, and my left hand worked under your dress, is it possible I wouldn't know it?"

"You mean the part of you that's talking to me now?"

"Yes. My left hemisphere."

"I don't think it would know that, no. Not if it didn't also intend to do that, and couldn't see the left hand."

"So if you told me in no uncertain terms to get my hand out from under your dress, I might be genuinely surprised?"

"Yes. The left side of your brain would be surprised."

"Now what if I said I didn't want any more to drink but my left hand signalled the bartender for another round?"

"You do sometimes get these conflicts, yes."

"Suppose I see my left hand doing something I don't want to do. Can I stop it?"

"Well, the speech hemisphere is usually dominant and has motor control, but not always."

"You mean I might not be able to stop it by exerting my will over that left hand?"

"That's correct."

"So what could I do? Nothing?"

"You might use your right hand to stop the left."

"You mean if I saw my left hand raising above your head to strike you, like this, my right hand might catch the left arm at the wrist and hold it back?"

"It could happen."

"Could I struggle so hard with my left arm as to leave bruises on the left wrist?"

"It's possible."

I heard an anguished sob behind me. When I turned to look, John Norton's head was bowed and his shoulders were quaking. Cindy put an arm around him.

"Thank you, Doctor Angell. Thank you very much."

"Your Honour." Carbonari wasn't so anxious to let Doctor Angell get back to her busy schedule after all. "If you please, I have a few questions remaining." The judge smiled and nodded.

4

"Doctor Angell, how many patients have you treated for this disease?"

"One."

"Is that all? Only the defendant?"

"It's a very rare disease, as I said before."

"Then how can you be sure all these things could happen? For example, that one hand might struggle with the other?"

"Intermanual conflicts like that are not uncommon in strokes or tumors affecting the corpus callosum, precisely because the two halves of the brain are then disconnected and the right hemisphere has a lot more independence than before."

"I see. But you also said you know of no personality differences between the hemispheres, didn't you?"

"Yes."

"Do you have any reason whatever to suppose the defendant suffers from a dissociation reaction, or multiple personality?"

"Not from what I've seen of him, no."

"Has that classical mental illness ever, in your knowledge, resulted from disconnecting the hemispheres of the brain?"

"No."

"It has not? Not ever?"

"I said no."

"Thank you. That will be all."

Judge Deakin peered at me quizzically. "Counsel for the Defence," he asked, "have you any further witnesses?"

I took a deep breath before answering, "Just one, your Honour."

"Well, I'm waiting. Who is it?"

"Defence calls John Norton to the stand."

Carbonari looked at me as if I were absolutely mad. I hoped he was wrong.

15. John Norton takes the stand

He got up slowly, looking almost as surprised as the Prosecutor. Cindy squeezed his hand reassuringly. I watched the other hand, the left one. From now on I would have to keep an eye on that hand all the time: it was the key to my defence.

I waited for the swearing-in to begin. Norton raised his right hand nervously; I could see the fingers trembling from twenty feet away. His voice came out awkwardly. "I do," he said. Fingers of the left hand were placed on the Bible all right, but they were tapping away nonchalantly, just as they had tapped on the Defence bench all through the trial. I glanced at the jurors to see if they noticed this. They hadn't, they were too intent on Norton's face. I'd have to find a way of getting them to watch that hand too.

"Mr. Norton, before you went to Doctor Greenspan for help, who knew you suffered from any illness?"

"Only Edith."

"Your wife?"

"Yes. She knew I couldn't eat properly because of a sore throat, that's all."

"Why did you give Doctor Greenspan a fake name?"

"I was afraid I was becoming epileptic because of the tremors I had."

"Did Mrs. Norton know you were being treated by Doctor Greenspan?"

"She knew I was seeing a doctor. But I gave her another name for the doctor, one I made up."

"Why?"

"So she wouldn't be able to talk to Doctor Greenspan about my condition. I was afraid he'd tell her the truth, that I had a progressive brain disease and might die."

"I see. And when Doctor Greenspan referred you to Doctor Angell, did you tell your wife about that?"

"No, for the same reason. I didn't even want her to know I had to go to a hospital. I was sure she'd find out the truth, and that it would kill her."

"But how did you conceal the treatments and throat surgery from her? Records show you spent three weeks in Rochester Hospital."

"I made up a story about going on a fishing trip to a remote place in Michigan. She believed me. Edith always believed me." His jaw started to tremble.

"But after the treatment, when you had recovered well and the disease was arrested, didn't you want to tell her then?"

"Not at first. I thought I'd wait a couple of months, to make sure I was cured. No point in raising false hopes. Then before the month was up these odd things started happening to me."

"What odd things? Take your time, now. Try to put everything in sequence."

"Well, I remember the first time very clearly. I was so pleased to be feeling well again, gaining back my weight and everything, that I began taking Edith out in the evenings.

I was still afraid, I admit it, but I had improved so much physically, with no sign of tremors, that Edith believed it had only been my throat condition which made me ill before. She spent every evening preparing tasty dishes for me so I would recover completely. So I decided to take her out that night . . . We went to a ballet performance together. Edith always loved . . ."

"How long was this after your treatment?"

"About six weeks after I left the hospital. So that would be, say, two months after the treatment. I remember I was secretly happy I could tell her the truth the very next week. I was thinking of that when it happened the first time."

"What happened?"

"I had the ballet programme open in my lap. There was a two-page photograph of a pretty ballerina in transparent tights leaping into the air. I turned the page to look at the programme of dances on the other side . . ."

"With which hand?"

"With my right hand. I'm right-handed."

"Go on."

"Then I leaned over to whisper something to Edith about a number she particularly liked when we saw it in New York several years before."

"She was seated where? To your right or left?"

"To my right."

"Continue."

"As I was whispering to her I saw a hand out of the corner of my eye reach over and turn the page back again."

"Back to the photograph of the ballerina?"

"Yes. I thought it was the man seated to my left, and I

remember getting annoyed at his nerve. After all, you don't look into someone else's programme without permission."

"So what did you do?"

"Without confronting him exactly—I'm not an aggressive person by nature—I simply flipped the page over again with my right hand, at the same time putting a finger on the dance number I was drawing Edith's attention to. I thought that would be hint enough."

"What happened then?"

"Well, I had withdrawn my finger so Edith could see the dance title. She complained she couldn't read it if I were going to turn the page on her. I looked down and sure enough, it was my own left hand that was doing the turning." A murmur spread just as Carbonari got to his feet.

"*Objection*. Witness is introducing unsupported evidence. By his own description no one else presently alive can support this testimony. Your Honour, he can tell us all kinds of things like this and . . ."

"*Overruled*, Mr. Carbonari. We have to get a little psychological depth here and there doesn't seem any other way. I'm willing to go some distance down this path, to see what facts it explains. Do you wish to record an exception?"

"Yes, your Honour."

"So be it. Continue, Mr. Shapman."

"Can you recall the next incident of this sort, Mr. Norton?"

"Yes. It was at work a few days later. I found I was having trouble with the book-keeping. Took me much longer to do than before."

"Would this be because your memory wasn't as good?"

"Yes. When I was carrying numbers from one column to the next, or even going down the same column, I'd keep forgetting what number it was and I'd have to start all over again. Eventually I found I had to enter each carried number in the margins as I went along, or use a calculator while I did it."

"Go on."

"Well, one day I was doing double-entries, with simple numbers on the left and complex ones in the right-hand column. I thought I'd do the complex ones first. As it happened I changed pencils, and was holding the other pencil in my left hand as I worked. I was concentrating so hard I didn't notice at first."

"Notice what?"

"What my left hand was doing. It was adding up the simple numbers in the left-hand column while I was doing the harder ones on the right." Another murmur rippled through the courtroom.

"Did you check these left-hand additions after you finshed the right-hand ones?"

"Yes. They were accurate."

"Same *Objection*," said Carbonari. "No substantiation."

"I am *overruling* for the same reason."

"Exception, your Honour."

"Let it be recorded. Carry on, Mr. Shapman."

"Mr. Norton, I believe playing chess is one of your hobbies. Is that correct?"

"Yes."

"When you play do you move pieces with your right or left hand?"

"Right hand. As I said, I'm right handed."

"After the operation did you continue to play with your right hand?"

"Of course."

"Let me put my question differently. After the operation were there any occasions when your left hand moved the pieces?"

He suddenly looked embarrassed. His head nodded up and down, but he didn't speak.

"It did sometimes move the pieces? Please answer, Mr. Norton."

"Yes."

"When was that?"

"Well, it happened once when I was at the club, a couple of weeks after the ballet I told you about. I was in a difficult end-game situation. I had little time left on the clock. I couldn't see how to Queen the Pawn in four moves. Suddenly my left hand advanced the King to brush away the opponent's King. It was the solution: I won easily."

"You mean you didn't decide to make that move yourself?"

"I didn't even consider it."

"Did you use the left hand to play games after that?"

"Not against others. I never played in competition again."

"You said not against others. Does that mean you started to play chess against yourself?"

"Sort of."

"How, exactly?"

"Well, after that game I couldn't wait to get home. I went straight back into the library and set up the pieces."

"You were alone?"

"Yes. Edith was upstairs sleeping. It was quite late."

"*Objection.*" Carbonari was doing this mechanically now. So was Judge Deakin.

"*Overruled.* Exception noted."

"How did you set up the pieces?"

"I was sitting to the side of the board, White pieces to my right, Black to my left. I moved White King's Pawn to King Four and waited."

"That was with your right hand?"

"Yes. Then the left hand moved the Black King's Pawn to King Three."

"You did not expect that move?"

"No. I always replied Black King's Pawn to King Four when playing Black pieces. I could see Black was going into the French Defence . . ."

"Which you were not familiar with?"

"Oh, I was familiar with it. But I didn't like it. I would never use it myself . . ."

"Mr. Norton, did White or Black win that game?"

His head bowed and he mumbled.

"Louder, Mr. Norton."

"Black won."

"You mean your left hand beat your right hand?"

"Yes. That's what I said." He sounded bitter about it.

"And did you play other games that way? How often?"

"Almost every night."

"Which hand won?"

"Well, I won some games . . ." Then it came out. He looked downcast, but a wildly inappropriate chuckle erupted from his mouth, followed by a look of surprise.

"How many games did your right hand win, Mr. Norton?"

"Two or three, anyway."

"Out of how many in all?" His head dropped again.

"Out of, I don't know, thirty or thirty-five."

"And your left hand won all the others?"

"There were a couple of draws."

I twisted around to glare at the Prosecutor. "Your witness," I snapped.

He came out of his chair hungrily. This would be it.

16. Introducing Henry

"Mr. Norton," began Carbonari, "you've been telling us about a lot of strange things you say happened to you which no one else witnessed or can tell us about. I'm going to ask you about things other people saw or experienced, things they say you did."

"I know."

"You know what?"

"What they say I did."

"Well, you'll have your chance to deny it. Let's start with Mrs. Vernon. She testified that you fondled her in the office several times. Is that true?"

"If I did I wasn't conscious of it."

"But you did fondle her?"

"I suppose I did. She says so. I don't think she'd make that up. She's a nice person. We always got on well together . . ."

"Then you admit you fondled her?"

"I must have. She was very upset at the time it happened."

"Do you remember the office party of September the first? When you and Mrs. Vernon were squeezed together against the bar?"

"Yes, I remember it." His face flushed.

"Did not Mrs. Vernon ask you to remove your hand from under her dress?"

"She did, all right. I was terribly embarrassed. We had just been chatting in a friendly way about Edith. About how much fun Edith had at the picnic."

"Did you in fact have your hand under her dress?"

"I don't know. I wasn't aware of it. I wouldn't do a dirty thing like that . . ."

"Was she lying, then?"

"Oh, no. She wouldn't . . ."

"Could she have been mistaken?"

"I doubt it. I know my left arm had been around her waist before."

"Were you drinking a lot?"

"I suppose so, at least for me."

"Where did you go after the party?"

"I started home . . ."

"Didn't you go to Clark and North Streets?"

"I don't know the names of the streets. But it was in that neighbourhood, yes."

"Did you accost a prostitute there?"

"Well, there was this woman standing at the corner. She had on a fur coat which she opened. She wore almost nothing underneath."

"Did you go to a room with her?"

"Yes . . . Yes, I did."

"Did you undress and get on the bed with her?"

"Yes."

"Did you attempt to have intercourse with her anally?"

"No. I've never done anything like that in my life. That's filthy!"

"Didn't she scream for help?"

"Yes, she screamed."

"Why would she scream, if you were just having intercourse with her normally? After all, that's what she agreed to do for the money, isn't it?"

"I suppose so."

"Didn't you try to strike her when she screamed?"

"No."

"Weren't your two hands raised above her in a threatening way?"

"Yes . . . yes, that's true."

"John Norton, on the night of October the twelfth, were you home alone the whole evening with your wife?"

"Yes. Until the police came."

"Why did the police come to your house?"

"Edith was screaming."

"Was she being hurt? Were you trying to have intercourse with her in the rectum?"

"No! God, I'd never do that with anyone. And I couldn't for the life of me hurt Edith . . ."

"Did you pick up this object"—he crossed to the exhibit table and picked up the paperweight—"in your left hand and strike Edith Norton with it about the head?"

"No . . . I just said . . ."

"Was this object in your left hand?"

"Yes. Yes, it was."

"And did it strike your wife?"

"Yes . . . It was horrible . . ."

"After that did you mount your wife's corpse and . . ."

"God, no! I couldn't have . . ."

"Thank you. No further questions, your Honour."

I decided to ask the same questions as Carbonari on my Re-direct, only with a different emphasis. But first there was one hurdle to clear.

"Mr. Norton, when you began playing chess against your left hand, did you begin to think of whomever it was controlling that hand as a different person?"

"Yes, I did."

"Did you ever talk to this person?"

"Well, he can't talk. But he understands a lot."

"You did sometimes, then, talk to him?"

"Yes."

"Did you call him by a name?"

"You can't talk to someone without using a name."

"What name did you use?"

"Henry."

I heard the Prosecutor sigh or scoff, I couldn't be sure which.

"Why did you use that name in particular?"

"Well, I was baptised John Henry Norton. I dropped the middle name years ago. I guess it seemed natural to use it . . ."

"Because you thought of him as yourself, or part of yourself?" This was the big question, but I wasn't sure how he'd answer.

"Well, sort of."

"What do you mean, sort of? Did you think of the person controlling your left hand as yourself, John Norton?"

"No! How could I? He was doing things with that hand I didn't want to do, and sometimes didn't know about."

"Then did you think of him as part of yourself?"

"In a way. After all, it was my hand he was moving . . ."

"Tell me, when Mrs. Vernon complained about you brushing up against her in the office, pinching her and so on, were you surprised?"

"Yes, I was."

"Since you were alone with her and didn't do it yourself . . ."

"*Objection*. Witness has already testified he did it."

"I withdraw my question, your Honour. Mr. Norton, since you were alone with her and were not aware of doing these things yourself, who did you think did them?"

"Henry." There it was at last, out into the open.

"And similarly the evening of September the first, when she accused you of having your hand under her dress?"

"Yes."

"You thought Henry had done it?"

"Of course I did."

"Did you say anything to Henry?"

"Your Honour," shouted the Prosecutor, "this is becoming ridiculous. He's leading the witness . . ."

"I don't agree, Mr. Carbonari. The questions are odd but straightforward. Let's hear the answers."

"Did you say anything?"

"I told him to stop that, yes. But only when we were alone. I didn't want people to think I was crazy, talking to myself."

"You mean *they* would think you were talking to yourself. But *you* didn't think you were talking to yourself, did you?"

"No."

"Did Henry ever answer? I mean, indicate he understood what you said to him?"

"He'd nod his head."

"*His* head?"

"Well, mine too. *Our* head."

"You mean you'd say something like, 'Don't ever do that again, Henry' and your head would nod up and down?"

"Yes."

"Without you wanting to nod it?"

"That's right." The jurors had their mouths open.

"Now when you left the office party did you intend driving home?"

"Yes."

"You had a lot to drink, you said. Why did you drink so much?"

"I didn't have much choice."

"Mrs. Vernon testified that you covered your glass when the bartender asked if you wanted another drink, and you said no."

"I did."

"With which hand did you cover the glass?"

"My right one."

"But at the same time you signalled for a fresh round with the other hand, the left one. Why did you do that?"

"I didn't. It was Henry."

"That's what you meant when you just said you didn't have much choice about drinking that evening?"

"Yes."

"Could Henry often make you do what you didn't want?"

"No, not usually. That was the first time. I felt I was trapped against the bar there, and it was only when Mrs. Vernon got angry I was able to break away . . ."

"You started driving home, you said, but you ended up at Clark and North Streets. How did that happen?"

"He kept twisting the wheel. I was afraid of an accident, so I let him drive."

"Henry?"

"Yes."

"Did you have any idea why he wanted to go to that neighbourhood?"

"Not at first. But when he pulled over to the kerb and braked . . ."

"Just a minute. *He* pulled over to the kerb and braked the car?"

"Yes. I have automatic transmission. When he braked with the left foot I had to take my foot off the accelerator."

"Go on."

"Then I saw this woman on the corner ahead, just standing there, waiting. At the same time I felt . . . well, do I have to tell this?"

"Yes, it's important."

"I felt I had an erection."

"Did you feel sexually excited?"

"A little. But I didn't want to do anything . . . He kept on pulling me. He opened the door and we got out."

"When the woman opened her coat to show her body, did that excite you?"

"Yes, I suppose it did. But I still wouldn't have . . ."

"Is that why when she asked you if you wanted 'the

Quickie' or 'all night' you shook your head from side to side?"

"Yes."

"That was *you* answering, not Henry?"

"Yes, but Henry reached in under her coat."

"The left hand?"

"Yes."

"So when she asked if you wanted 'the Special' and your head nodded 'yes' it was Henry answering."

"Definitely."

"Did you know what 'the Special' meant?"

"No, I didn't."

"Did you have any idea what Henry wanted as a Special?"

"Not then."

"Were you surprised when Henry signalled for her to turn over on the bed?"

"Yes. I don't like that. It's degrading."

"You mean having intercourse from the rear?"

"Yes."

"Were you not excited anyway?"

"I've already told you . . . yes, how could I not be with an erection?"

"Were you surprised when Henry guided the penis towards her rectum?"

"I didn't notice that until she screamed. Then Henry pulled her top leg back and kept trying to insert it . . . She screamed louder. I saw my left arm go up above her head as if to strike her. I grabbed it with my right hand. We struggled."

"*Who* struggled?"

"Henry and I. Then he got frightened. I felt all the

strength go out of him. I took over everything. I got dressed quickly . . ."

"When you say you took over everything, do you mean you could control your left hand again?"

"Yes. Everything. I ran down the stairs and drove home. Edith had been worried . . ."

"Did Henry ever gain control over your body like that again?"

"Just once."

"When was that?"

"On October the twelfth. The night Edith died."

17. The Night Edith died

"John Norton," I said, "I am going to have to ask you some painful and embarrassing questions about that night, but you must do your best to answer them. Will you promise me to do that?"

"I will."

"Thank you. Tell me about your married life before October the twelfth. Were you and your wife happy together?"

"Very much so."

"Sexually, too?"

"Well, Edith was never sexually demanding. Some people might say she was cold. And I had my health to worry about in later years. But on the whole we were well-matched, I'd say."

"Was there any change after your illness and tremors set in?"

"Yes, but that was my fault. Partly I think it was the weakness due to starvation, partly my self-disgust after a blackout. I couldn't help wondering how Edith could bear to kiss my mouth if it ever started frothing—you see, I thought I was becoming epileptic."

"So you did not have much of a sex life the last months before your treatments?"

"No, we didn't."

"Would you say you made love twice a week, every week—how often?"

"Every couple of weeks would be more like it. Edith was always willing, but as I said, she didn't press."

"Thank you. Did your recovery change things in that respect?"

"Yes, it did. I was eating well again, and as I was beginning to lose fear of the disease coming back . . ."

"So you found greater happiness in that way?"

"Not exactly."

"What do you mean? Please be frank."

"Well, it wasn't just the frequency that changed. Last summer . . ."

"About the time you were alleged to have made advances on Mrs. Vernon?"

"Yes, beginning then I found myself doing things, and asking things of Edith that I wouldn't have dared before."

"Could you be explicit here? I know it's embarrassing, but . . ."

"Well, once when she was kissing me I found I was pushing her head down, down my chest and stomach . . ."

"Towards your penis?"

"Yes. I had never suggested that to her before."

"Did she respond?"

"I'm . . . I'm afraid she did . . . She said something like, 'Oh, John' and 'Do you want me to?', but she did it."

"She took your organ in her mouth?"

"Yes."

"Were you repelled by this?"

"No. It was very pleasant. But I never would have asked it of her. In fact I said that was enough, but she kept on with it. Then I realised my hand was holding her head down there."

"Your left hand?"

"Yes. The same hand that pushed her down there. You see the lights were out—we always kept the lights off—and I couldn't feel that hand any more."

"You realised Henry had done it?"

"Of course."

"How did you react to this?"

"What could I do? I didn't want Edith to know it wasn't me. She would have been horrified. I pulled the hand with my right hand, that's all. Pulled it away."

"Did she then stop?"

"No . . . No, she kept right on."

"For how long?"

"Until I . . . until it was over."

"You mean she enjoyed doing it?"

"Apparently. Yes, she must have. She did it often after that."

"Mr. Norton, were you sexually jealous of Henry?"

"I don't know . . . perhaps."

"Did he attempt other things?"

"Yes. When I wasn't watching I'd find that left hand behind her in bed, fondling her to get her excited. And sometimes she complained I was hurting her there too, though I didn't know it . . ."

"You mean your left hand was between her buttocks?"

"Yes, that's what I mean."

"Mr. Norton, what happened the night of October the twelfth?"

"It was a nightmare I don't want to relive."

"Let me help you, then. Did Henry attempt the same

sort of sexual assault on your wife that he had tried with Rosa Paguera?"

"He certainly did."

"How could he, since you were careful to watch out for what the left hand was up to?"

"Do I have to go into detail?"

"It would be a great help."

"Well, I was lying on top of Edith. I had my right arm under her neck, my face buried in her breasts. I couldn't see the left hand, but since Edith was lying on her back I didn't worry . . ."

"Go on."

"I slipped out. I felt a hand seize my penis to put it back in again. I thought it was Edith's hand, which was silly since she didn't have any hand on that side. She raised her thighs to grip me around the back. I felt it going in again. She said, 'John, please don't. It's too big.' I didn't understand. I felt terribly squeezed . . ."

"You mean your penis?"

"Yes. It hurt me too. But my hips started thrusting hard. I realised I hadn't wanted to move with such force. Edith screamed."

"What did you do?"

"I pulled myself away. I slid off the bed. I fumbled for the light switch. It was on a night table several feet from the bed. There was an onyx paperweight alongside the lamp. When the light went on I was looking at Edith. She was crying and frightened. I asked what happened. She moaned and held her, her . . ."

"Buttocks?"

"Yes."

"She was to your right?"

"Yes. I moved towards her in the light. Her eyes grew wide with terror. I followed her eyes. The paperweight was in my left hand. I moved to take it away, but the hand raised quickly. I was standing next to Edith now. I realised what he was going to do. I reached up and caught the left wrist in my right hand fingers . . . Edith was screaming wildly."

"Weren't you able to hold it?"

"No. I squeezed with all my strength, but he was like a maniac. The wrist pulled backwards. At the same time he must have pushed with the left leg, because I was pitched sideways on to the bed. I lost my grip. He smashed her forehead with the stone. Blood came out of her nostrils. He struck again and again . . ."

"Please, Mr. Norton. Pull yourself together."

"It was . . . awful."

"What happened then?"

"The rest is like a dream. Edith was dead. I couldn't believe it. I was stunned. I could offer no resistance any more. He pushed back her leg. He took her hand off the buttocks. He slipped a pillow under her hip, pushing with the left shoulder to raise her hips. Then . . . no . . . no, I can't go on . . ."

"I think that is quite enough, Mr. Norton. I'm sorry I put you through this." I glanced at Carbonari. He shook his head, signifying he had no questions.

"Are you finished with the witness, Mr. Shapman?" It was Judge Deakin, as cool and unperturbed as always. I stopped half-way back to my bench. I had an idea.

"Not quite, your Honour." I whirled around to face the witness box, "John Norton," I said. He sat up abruptly.

"I have a further question. My last one. But I don't

want you to say anything. And I particularly don't want you to move any part of your body. Is that clear?" He sat there stolidly, waiting for it. His right hand was relaxed, composed. Fingers of the left hand drummed softly on the edge of the witness box, in full view of the jury.

"*Henry,*" I shouted, "*Did* you *kill Edith Norton?*" The fingers stopped drumming. Norton looked at them. Everyone followed his eyes. "*Did you?*" They clenched into a fist. "*Well, Answer: did you or did you not kill Edith Norton?*"

The hand turned upside down. The middle finger extended at me lewdly. Then it dropped, and Norton's head nodded slowly up and down.

"Your Honour," I said, "the Defence rests."

18. In the Judge's chambers

"Well, gentlemen, it's been an exhausting day. Please make yourselves comfortable."

Arthur Deakin took off his robes, gestured to us to be seated, and busied himself hanging the robes on a tall stand behind his chair. I collapsed in the thick leather, of unaccustomed softness. George Carbonari offered me a cigar, but I declined. The judge fidgeted with a carafe and tiny glasses on his desk.

"You must try this sherry. I insist. It's English, but of course made in Spain. You know where the best Spanish sherry comes from? Near a little village in the southern part called Jerez de la Frontera. Miriam and I—that's Mrs. Deakin—visited there last winter. Pronounced Hair-ETH. How the English corrupted that into 'sherry' I'll never understand. But by any name it tastes just as good. There you are . . ." He settled back and ran his tongue along the outer edge of his upper lip. "Ahh . . ."

"Now, gentlemen, to the gravamen of the matter. You wonder why I summoned you. It's very simple. To-morrow you are to give your summations. I may be able to spare you that oratical ordeal."

"Oh?" I sat up quickly.

"I may. On the other hand I may not."

Carbonari stirred. "I think I know what you have in mind, Arthur, and I can't say I like it."

"That's what we're here for, George. I want your reactions in advance. And Mr. Shapman's."

"Could I be let in on this?" I still didn't know what he was planning.

"Yes," he said, putting his glass down very precisely. "I'm thinking of a directed verdict." He dabbed at his lips with a corner of his handkerchief before continuing. "Of directing the jury to find John Norton not guilty by reason of insanity. But let's have George's views first."

"I don't like it."

"You said that. Why not?"

"It implies I did not offer evidence of sanity. But I did. Temperton's perfectly competent . . ."

"He didn't know Norton's brain was disconnected when he examined him."

"No, but Doctor Angell found no serious change, and she's the expert here."

"True, but she didn't know of all these conflicts developing."

"How do we know they did? We've only got his word for it."

"So you would appeal on grounds that I allowed Norton's unsupported testimony as evidence?"

"I might. I'd have to think about it. In any case I think you should let the jury decide whether they believe him."

"Even then I could reverse if I wanted."

"You could, but I don't believe you would, Arthur."

"Probably not, if it got that far. I'd expect Mr. Shapman to appeal and let appellate court decide for or against reversal. My question is whether I should let it get that far. But I admit I'm reluctant to take a capital case with such dramatic overtones away from the jury."

"Just a minute," I said. "Can you enter a directed verdict if the defendant made no request for it?"

"I could, yes. I'm assuming you will make an insanity plea in your summation tomorrow. I might save you the trouble."

"On what grounds?" It was Carbonari butting in without giving me a chance to state my intentions.

"What grounds?" Deakin looked surprised.

"The McNaghten Rule is satisfied. He himself testified he knew what was going on and that it was wrong."

"Yes," said the judge, "but could he prevent it?"

"Bah!" Carbonari blew smoke in my direction. "Sonny Boy here made a lot of noise about left hand, right hand, but the only evidence we've got is the accused's own statements."

"Oh come now, George. Doctor Angell admitted such conflicts occur. And there was plenty of support for odd behaviour—like his looking surprised and it being out of character when he had that hand on Mrs. Vernon's exquisite posterior. In *Durham versus the United States*, Judge Bazelon took it as a fundamental principle that the mind of man is a functional unit. Thus he can't be only partially diseased. The whole personality is affected."

"Yes, but in the American Law Institute formulation, which supersedes *Durham*, Rule Two provided that 'mental disease or defect' does not cover an abnormality manifested solely by repeated criminal or anti-social conduct."

"I doubt that ALI applies here. Besides, it's been much

criticised for assuming just what *Durham* tried to exclude, the idea of a compartmentalised mind."

"It's the law in Illinois, Arthur."

"The truth is we don't have a satisfactory legal definition of insanity."

"All the more reason to let the jury handle it."

"I suppose so." Judge Deakin sighed, took another sip of sherry and looked at me. "Well, young man, it looks like I won't be able to help you out after all. It's up to you to convince them your man is off his rocker."

"Thanks, but no thanks."

"What do you mean?"

"I have no intention of offering an insanity defence for John Norton. His body has a compartmentalised mind, but he doesn't."

Judge Deakin put the glass down with a sharp "clink". Carbonari held his cigar butt poised half-way to his mouth. I waited. The Prosecutor said it first.

"What in Christ's Heaven kind of defence *are* you going to offer? You're going to deny he did it when he's admitted it on the stand?"

"He did not admit it. In fact he denied it. He said Henry did it. And I believe him."

"Mr. Shapman." Deakin's kindly old eyes were still widening. "Do I understand you intend to argue your client is *not* Henry, as well as John, Norton?"

"That is correct." I stood up and began to button my jacket. "And John Norton is not insane. Henry may be, but I'm not defending him."

They got to their feet too. I felt like being flippant.

"See you in court tomorrow, gentlemen. And thanks for the *jerez*."

Part 3: Summations

19. For the Defence

I watched the jury members file in and take their seats in the box. Carbonari was looking at me with a quizzical smile on his face, wondering no doubt how I thought I was going to pull this off. Cindy's note read, not "Good luck", but "Break a leg". I thought it appropriate.

As we rose for Judge Deakin's entry and the bailiff's call to order I scanned the jury's faces once more. There must be one, I thought, just one member who could put himself into John Norton's shoes. If I could find him I'd strap those shoes on so tight the other eleven would never get them off. But then what would I have? A hung jury? A new trial, this time without surprises? If I did, Carbonari would put ten new experts on the stand to show you could divide a human brain four ways and still have the same person. I remained standing as everyone eased back into his seat. Judge Deakin nodded to me to begin. I felt terribly alone.

"Ladies and gentlemen," I began, "Edith Norton was murdered and her corpse violated. The defendant was in the room with her when these things happened. His left hand held the murder weapon when it was used to kill her. His body raped her corpse."

The jury's eyes widened as I approached. I could see they were confused. Was I taking the Prosecutor's rôle?

5

"It must seem to you that if he, John Norton, did these things he did them insanely, under some terrible compulsion. After all, he had no rational motive. There was no insurance on her life, there was no other woman, and we know he loved her all those years. What is more, he made no attempt to escape. He just sat there by her body, waiting for the police to break down the door, shut off a burglar alarm and come upstairs through an unlocked door and find him sitting there, muttering 'Poor Edith, poor Edith'.

"But then there are those bruises on his left wrist. Remember them? Sergeant Devereux was very precise about those. They could only have been made by someone's right hand squeezing or holding that wrist very hard. Holding it back, trying to prevent that hand from smashing the paperweight into Edith Norton's face and head. Now *whose* right hand did that? Not Mrs. Norton's, because she had no right hand. She lost hers in a childhood accident. Then who else tried to save her life? According to Sergeant Devereux there was no third person in that room at the time, because no fingerprints or footprints other than John and Edith Norton's were found. In fact, ladies and gentlemen, there was only *one* right hand in that room, the defendant John Norton's. Only *his* right hand could have struggled with the left hand to save his wife's life.

"If so, if this is the only possible explanation, was he not insane? I say *no*. I say no because there has not been a shred of evidence introduced in testimony to suggest an insane person might try to physically prevent *himself* from carrying out an insane act. No, John Norton was not insane. He did not kill his wife insanely. He did not ravage her dead body insanely. He did none of these things insanely," I paused, "because he did not do them at all."

A whisper started in the courtroom. Members of the jury sat back abruptly, as if I had slapped a dozen faces at once. The Prosecutor picked up his pencil to make a note, shaking his head from side to side incredulously. I turned away from the jury box, then spun back quickly.

"Ladies and gentlemen, Sergeant Devereux was wrong. There *was* a third person in the bedroom that fatal night. But the police could not be expected to detect his presence, because he has the same footprints, the same fingerprints, as John Norton. When you look at the defendant, you are looking at him too. But he is not John Norton. He is a different man, with a different personality.

"Do not misunderstand me, ladies and gentlemen. I am not saying my client has a multiple personality. That would be the basis for an insanity plea, but I am not offering one. John Norton always had the same personality. The murderer and rapist had a different personality. How do we know this? We know it because in multiple personality different personalities *succeed* each other. The victim of this disorder thinks of himself as one person today, another tomorrow or next week. He does not feel he is two persons *at the same time*. He does not fight for control of his own body. The defendant did not become another person, kill his wife, violate her corpse, and then revert to himself. If he had he could not have struggled to prevent these things happening. But he did try to prevent them. Those bruises on the left wrist prove it."

I walked away towards the Defence table to get a drink of water, but really to let those words sink in. When I walked back I had my hands in my pockets, as if what I had just argued must be plain to everyone.

"Of course if we had to rely on the defendant's testimony alone, you might have doubts about all this. Fortunately we do not. We also have the expert testimony of Doctor Angell, who treated him and who confirmed Doctor Greenspan's guess that the halves of his brain were disconnected.

"Remember the words she used when Mr. Carbonari asked her if this radical disconnection, this eating away of the nerve connections between the two hemispheres of the brain, if this could cause a sexual perversion to develop? She said no, because separating the hemispheres does not *add* to what's already there in each hemisphere. Notice she did not say there was nothing in one of the hemispheres which, when no longer so controlled by the other, might not result in developing a sexual perversion, but just that if there were, the disease did not put it there.

"Then she went on to draw this parallel. She said the effect of the disease is like disconnecting Siamese twins. Neither twin is changed by being freed from the other. But she added, and these are her very words, 'Of course the difference here is that Siamese twins have two bodies to begin with, while the hemispheres control the same body.' If we are going to take her testimony seriously, and I remind you Doctor Angell is an expert witness, each hemisphere is basically an independent person, just the same way Siamese twins are, except that they control a single body.

"Now look at the Prosecutor's next questions to her in that light. He asked if separation of the defendant's brain hemispheres could have prevented him from knowing the nature and quality of any act he may have performed after this took place. She said no. He then asked if it could have prevented him from having the power or control over his will to avoid committing that act. She said no again.

"But *whom* are we talking about here? The defendant is John Norton. He talks, so *his* brain after the operation would be the left hemisphere, where the speech centres are. The hand *he* normally controls is the right hand. That is not the hand that killed Edith Norton. It is the hand that tried to prevent her death. The hand that killed his wife despite his attempts to prevent it was sometimes controlled by a different person, whose brain is the right hemisphere and to whom John Norton gave the name Henry."

I broke off and went back to the Defence table for another drink of water. Cindy Adams crossed fingers of both hands and nodded encouragingly. I didn't dare look at John. When I turned around two of the male jurors were looking thoughtfully at their left hands. I walked to the exhibit table and stopped there, my fingers drumming on it the way John Norton's had when he was on the witness stand.

"Doctor Angell also testified that if I had this disease and were staring straight ahead at you I wouldn't see anything to my left, at least until my eyes had time to scan the room. Now what if one of you were my beloved wife and started screaming while I was making love to you? The room is dark so I come over here to turn on the light." I reached above the table to turn on an imaginary lamp, still staring at the jurors. "The light goes on but you are moaning in pain and I am looking directly at you, frightened and wondering what is the matter.

"According to Doctor Angell my left hand could pick up an object like this one," I said while seizing the stone paperweight in the fingers of the left hand, "and I would not know I had done so. I could then advance on you, concerned to see what's wrong, and be surprised to see you looking to my left, eyes widened with terror, looking above my head to the left of me and suddenly screaming."

I was standing at the edge of the jury box now, the heavy stone wavering in my hand above three or four jurors' heads. One, a thin old lady, involuntarily raised her arms.

"Doctor Angell testified that in such circumstances, where I suddenly see my left hand is trying to do something I do not want, I might reach up with my other hand, like this, and seize the wrist to prevent it." I put up my right hand and pretended to struggle. Then I relaxed and walked back to the exhibit table, letting the stone fall heavily on it. "That would account for bruises on my left wrist, would it not?"

I shot a quick look at the jurors. The thin old lady was nodding her head slowly.

"Now what does all this mean? *Who* picked up the stone? Who raised it to strike you? How could *I*, the talkative young lawyer you are listening to, be the person who did these things? *I* didn't know it was in my left hand. *I* didn't even see it until it was raised to strike you. When I did see it I tried to stop it by seizing that wrist.

"But *someone* did. Who, if not me? The answer can

only be the person who wanted to kill you in order to rape you. The person who, unlike me, does not talk, though he understands. The silent murderer and rapist. That person is not me. It is not John Norton. *My* brain, and the defendant's, is this one, the left hemisphere. *His* is the speechless right hemisphere. But he is not charged with murder. John Norton is."

I took a deep breath and planted myself firmly in front of the jury box. This would be my final argument. I started softly, so they would have to strain to hear me.

"Suppose *you* had this disease, ladies and gentlemen. Suppose you find your left hand doing things you don't intend to do, don't approve of, don't always know it's doing until too late, sometimes can't prevent. Would you feel morally or legally responsible for these things?"

I raised my voice a notch.

"Suppose your right hemisphere becomes more and more dominant. Suppose you find it can outplay you at games. Suppose it sometimes forces you to drive a car where you don't want to go."

Now I moved up two notches, advancing slowly but threateningly and thinking Cindy was right—if I lost this case I could always try a stage career.

"Suppose one horrible night you find that hemisphere trying to force someone you love more than anyone in the world into a perverse sexual act. You fight to control that side of your body. You cannot. There is a struggle and before your very eyes that loved one is bludgeoned to death. Then, could there be anything more terrible? You are forced to commit that act on her corpse, though your own feeling is one of despair and anguish. Can you imagine that, ladies and gentlemen?"

I was shouting now, driving at them with all I had.

"*Would you feel guilty for what part of your body did? Would you plead guilty to murder?*"

I let my voice drop back almost to a whisper.

"Members of the jury, if your answer to these questions is no, you must not add to John Norton's suffering. You must find him innocent and set him free.

"Thank you."

George Carbonari brushed past me contemptuously to get to the jury box. He stood at one corner and talked simply and directly to them, in contrast to my theatrics. Reason, I could see, was going to prevail over emotion if he had his way. And as I listened I thought he'd won.

20. For the Prosecution

"Well, ladies and gentlemen, you heard an interesting argument from Defence counsel this morning. Now let's get down to hard facts.

"Someone killed and raped Edith Norton. No one denies that. That someone is in fact in this courtroom. No one denies this, either. He is sitting over there at the Defence table. His left hand there, the one drumming on the table, held this stone paperweight and smashed it into her face while she screamed with terror. All this is accepted as fact by counsel for the Defence.

"Now who is that man? His legal name is John Norton. It once was John Henry Norton, but we'll skip that. According to Mr. Shapman, John Norton is not insane. He never suffered from a personality disorder and does not now. I agree. Then is he not responsible for the murder of his wife?

"No, says Mr. Shapman. He is not because *he* did not do it. Indeed he tried to prevent it. Then *who* did it? Oh, says Mr. Shapman, Henry did it. And who is Henry? Is he in this room? Yes! *Where* is he? Under the table, or hiding behind John Norton? No, he *is* John Norton. He is a different person sharing and sometimes controlling the body John Norton has, but he is not John Norton. That is the real culprit, not our benevolent defendant here.

"Members of the jury, what kind of nonsense is this? Do you believe it? Why was Edith Norton murdered? Was it not to abuse her carnally, in an unnatural way she would not permit otherwise? And when her brains were smashed so blood ran through her nose—the defendant himself gave us that description—who abused her? Did Henry do it, not John Norton? Ah, but this time there was no right hand, left hand. The defendant has, we may trust, but one penis, and he admitted he got sexual pleasure when it was erect.

"On the witness stand John Norton broke down, or seemed to break down, when he was asked to describe what happened *after* his left hand tore free of the right one and delivered those fatal blows. It was too horrible, he said, to recount. Now you might—I said you *might*—be tempted to believe his story up to that point. But can you believe, you male jurors, can you believe you would get sexual pleasure from penetrating a corpse's rectum to the point of ejaculating therein, while feeling extreme *revulsion*? I don't think you can imagine it. And you lady jurors, could you believe your husband or son if he told you he raped a woman that way while feeling intense *disgust*?

"Mr. Shapman has been very attentive to Doctor Angell's testimony. He made a lot of her analogy with Siamese twins. But she never said the separated hemispheres are two *persons*. That is the interpretation Defence counsel wants to foist upon you. In fact when Mr. Shapman asked her if he were squeezed up against her in a crowded bar and had his left hand under Doctor Angell's dress, would he know it, she answered as follows: 'You mean *the part of you* that's talking to me now?'

In other words the left hemisphere does the talking, the right recognises faces and so on, but they are both parts *of the same person*, even when disconnected. So Mr. Shapman's left hemisphere might not know what the left hand is up to, but Mr. Shapman's right hemisphere would. It's still Mr. Shapman. *He* is one person and responsible for anything either hemisphere or hand does.

"Again, Defence counsel said Doctor Angell testified that conflicts do sometimes develop between the two hemispheres. Yes, she said that. But she did *not* say John Norton had developed such conflicts. She gave no evidence at all to that effect. She merely responded to hypothetical questions posed by Mr. Shapman. In her own experience of the defendant there was nothing abnormal except the partial amnesia she described. So far as she *knows*, there are no personality differences between the hemispheres. In any case, patients who have had this kind of cerebral disconnection do not *develop* sexual perversions. They do not kill their loved ones in order to ravish the corpse. Defence counsel has not produced one scintilla of expert testimony to support his claim that the defendant did what he did because of the disease he had.

"No, the only testimony we have heard to that effect comes not from an expert witness, but from the defendant himself. If you are going to believe he, John Norton, did not know, or when he knew could not prevent, doing the things he did, you can rely only on what he said. Did his left hand turn the ballet programme? We don't know. Edith Norton was there, but she is now dead. Did he play chess with himself and lose to his left hand? Again, we don't know. Was he able to add up two columns of figures simultaneously with each hand?

Who knows? He seems to have done certain parts of the intelligence test with his left hand, but why should we believe he is normally right-handed? Maybe he is, but we have only his word for it. He may be ambidextrous, as Doctor Temperton said he was.

"Did John Norton not know his left hand pinched Mrs. Vernon, or later tried to drive fingers between her buttocks? She testified that he looked surprised when she accused him of these things, but of course any old lecher can feign surprise. I'm not saying he lied. I'm merely saying we have no way of telling if he told the truth. In Anglo-Saxon jurisprudence the accused is not required to testify against himself. That does not mean that when he agrees to testify we must accept everything he says.

"Did another person drive the car to Clark and North Streets the night of September the first? Did another person proposition Miss Paguera? Did another person go up to her room with her, undress himself, ask her to turn over on the bed and try to penetrate her buttocks? Again there was only one erect penis, and one known person trying to do this—John Norton.

"Counsel for Defence made much also of a struggle between the left and right hands of the defendant. He suggested to Miss Paguera that one was trying to hold the other back. But *she* didn't notice that. Her words were these: 'One hand held the other wrist, like they were forming a club.' That is a very precise eye-witness description. If it was true in her experience, could it not be equally true of the hands that held the murderous paper-weight above Edith Norton's head? A club, but this time a deadly stone-weighted club? But unfortunately we cannot have Edith Norton's testimony. She is gone for ever.

"Now I come to the most difficult part of my summation. If in spite of everything I have been saying you are convinced by Mr. Shapman's argument, think of the consequences. The defendant had his brain hemispheres separated. In Doctor Angell's words, *nothing was added to them* by this separation. That implies nothing is subtracted from either hemisphere by the fact that they are normally joined. A person remains one and the same person, whether his cerebral hemispheres are joined or separated.

"In that case, to take as a legitimate defence in John Norton's case that his brain was disconnected—but not claim insanity as a result of this—can only mean he is, and *always was*, just his left hemisphere: the one that does the talking. Which implies he was never his right hemisphere. This he dominated before: now it is free to do what *it* wants, independently of his knowledge and will. But if so, might it not do the same even when joined to the left hemisphere? Might it not at least assert its will and sometimes overpower the left hemisphere *without* disconnection?

"Reflect on these implications. Think what it means to the administration of criminal justice. If you find John Norton innocent of the murder and sodomitic violation of his wife's body because he was not the person who did these things, why could not any future murderer excuse himself on the same grounds? Why could he not say, 'It wasn't me, it was James, or Stephen, or Benjamin, who did it'? He wouldn't even have to have had the disease. It would be enough to hold the murder weapon in his left hand: it would be enough to guide his penis with that same left hand.

"Ladies and gentlemen, you are not irresponsible. You do not want to be recalled for jury service five years from now and hear a confessed criminal admit he committed a capital offence with part of his brain, with one of his hands, and with part of his sexual organ—all these belonging to some separate person.

"If you are not irresponsible and do not want to see this happen, you will do your duty under the laws of our State. You will find John Norton guilty of murder in the first degree.

"Thank you."

A hush fell over the courtroom. George Carbonari snapped his fingers as he sauntered by our table, as if to say, "See how easy it is when you have the last word?"

But he didn't have the last word. Judge Deakin did, and after him the jury itself.

Part 4: The Verdict

21. Instructions to the jury

"Members of the jury, this is the time when I, as judge of these trial proceedings, am charged to instruct you in the law governing this case. It is of course for you, not me, to determine how to apply the law to evidence and testimony you have heard. If I say anything, or it appears to you the Court has said something, that indicates a view as to what your determination of the facts should be, you must immediately disregard such a statement.

"The defendant is charged with murder in the first degree. This means he is said to have killed his wife wilfully and with malice aforethought, and while of sound mind and body. The Prosecution also accuses him of violating her person in an unnatural way after killing her. However that is not part of the capital charge against him. Rather this is to be understood as a contributory cause or motive for the murder.

"In order to find the defendant guilty of murder in the first degree you must be satisfied, first that he killed Edith Norton and second, that he did not do so accidentally or insanely or in self-defence or by entrapment.

"Let us consider the second requirement before the first. From Sergeant Devereux's testimony it is obvious the killing was no accident—Mrs. Norton's screams were heard by neighbours and she was repeatedly struck with a heavy object about the face and head. Furthermore, Doctor Fahy testified that she had been raped rectally after her death, though here you may feel his autopsy was not reliable, as adduced by Counsel for Defence on cross-examination. Doctor Greenspan did leave an opening for accidental death in testifying that the defendant was subject to some kind of minor convulsions, but he was careful to deny they were epileptic and Doctor Angell in any case testified they had an organic basis which was cured long before the killing took place.

"As for self-defence, or being led unintentionally to kill his wife, no one has suggested this was the case, and you can afford to overlook it.

"This leaves insanity as a possible defence. Mr. Shapman has eschewed that line of defence, and Mr. Carbonari of course concurs. Both contending parties hold John Norton to have been sane at the time Edith Norton died. However it is open to you to find differently. You might determine that the defendant did not know the nature or quality of his act at the time or, knowing it, could not resist doing what you think he did. If this is what you determine you will have found him not guilty by reason of insanity. In that case I should be obliged to order his indefinite commitment to a hospital for the criminally insane.

"Now we come to the first and only remaining requirement of a verdict of murder in the first degree, namely whether or not it was John Norton who killed her.

"This will be your most difficult task, because neither contending party denies John Norton's was the only other body present in the room when Edith Norton died. Neither party denies his hand wielded the weapon that killed her. Neither party denies that the act was done wilfully, and with malicious purpose, namely to abuse her body carnally.

"The contention of Defence counsel is that John Norton did none of these things because his brain was not controlling the hand that killed his wife, nor even the penis which subsequently violated her body. On the contrary, it is argued by Defence that another brain— and that is what Defence holds to be a result of the disease Doctor Angell described—was controlling the parts of John Norton's body which did these things, and that he tried to prevent them with the parts he could still control.

"Note, however, that we are here on entirely new legal grounds. For what Defence claims is that two distinct *persons* existed in and controlled at times different parts of the same human body. There is no legal precedent whatever for this construction being placed upon the facts.

"That does not mean you are forbidden to place such a construction upon them. New precedents are being established all the time in the law, which is like an ever-changing organic growth. However you should not do so lightly.

"You must determine, in view of all this, whether John Norton killed his wife on October the twelfth, and if so was sane at the time, or whether someone else then controlling his left hand did so.

"I leave you now to your deliberations."

22. The Execution of Henry Norton

I watched the clock's hands march around their appointed stations with agonising slowness. Only two hours had gone by; why had we rushed through lunch, just to sit here and look at a clock? Cindy leaned over and whispered:

"It's better for us if they take a long time."

"Why?"

"Because that shows they're arguing about interpretation, not the facts. The facts are too straightforward to spend a couple of hours on."

"That doesn't tell us how the argument will end."

"I predict a split jury. The women will take your side, the men Carbonari's."

"Why? He's better-looking than I am."

"Yes, but you're nicer."

"Thanks."

"Besides, women have more imagination than men. And they don't think their backsides are as sacrosanct as men make out."

"Cindy, you're projecting."

"No, I'm not. I'll bet you half the women on that jury . . ."

"Hold it. They're coming out."

The foreman came first. What was his name again?

Bolton? Yolton? Something like that. He looked very unhappy. Maybe Cindy was right and we had a hung jury. God, I thought, let's hope not. That would be worse than a guilty verdict. At least I could appeal that. But with a hung jury we'd have to go through the whole trial again . . . We were rising for Judge Deakin now. He seemed nervous. Probably wished he'd never been mixed up in this thing. So did I.

"Mr. Foreman, do you have a verdict?"

"We do not, your Honour."

"You do not? Why not?"

"We need further instruction from you before reaching a verdict."

"On what matter do you need further instruction?"

"If it pleases the Court," he said, pausing to glance at a note in his hand, "we wish to know if Henry Norton could be indicted for the murder of Edith Norton should we find the defendant not guilty."

A buzzing sound spread through the courtroom. I sighed in relief; Cindy squeezed my arm with joy; Carbonari threw me a bitter look. Judge Deakin let his mouth sag, then snapped it shut in obvious displeasure.

"There is no legal person named Henry Norton. That is a name used by defendant to describe acts of the right cerebral hemisphere. I do not think the Prosecutor would attempt to indict the defendant under another name: by the logic of his own argument in summation that would be charging the same man twice for the same crime.

"No, if the jury is convinced John Norton was not the person who killed his wife, you must simply find him not guilty. Does that answer your question?"

"Yes, it does, your Honour."

"Do you wish to retire again to reach a verdict?"

"If it pleases the Court, I think we have now reached one."

"And what is that verdict?"

"Not guilty."

Pandemonium broke out in the courtroom. We were being mobbed at the Defence table; Judge Deakin was gavelling everyone into silence, but I could hear nothing. I was too busy shouting into Cindy Adams' lovely ear.

"We did it! I thought they wanted to be sure somebody paid for the crime. I thought that with the judge's instruction they might go back and find him guilty in the first degree. But no! They were going for insanity if Carbonari could indict him again. Don't you see, Cindy? They wanted to *protect* him, to make sure John wouldn't be punished for . . ." Deakin was shouting louder than me.

"Silence! I will have silence in this Court. Bailiff, get those people back to their seats. Otherwise I'll clear the courtroom."

The hubbub died down. The judge turned back towards the jury.

"Ladies and gentlemen, I want to thank you for your services. It was a difficult trial, and I am sure you have done your duty with an eye to nothing but justice. You are dismissed. Will the defendant please rise?"

John's chair scraped the floor noisily as he stood up. A complete hush fell over the courtroom. It was as if he were standing alone in the eye of a storm, and in a sense he was.

"Mr. Norton, you have been tried and acquitted of murder in the first degree by a jury of your peers. You are free to go as you . . ."

"It's not fair." I pulled at his sleeve.

"What? I didn't catch that."

"I said it's not fair."

The judge looked startled.

"I'm afraid I don't understand, Mr. Norton. You have been found innocent . . ."

"What about Henry? Is he going to get off scot free? Am I going to have to live with him the rest of my life knowing what he did to Edith?" His voice was rising rapidly now.

"Please, Mr. Norton. Calm yourself."

"*I tell you it's not fair. He's laughing at me right now. He'll laugh at me all the rest of my life . . .*"

"Bailiff, please take Mr. Norton out of the Court."

"*He's dangerous, your Honour. You think he won't do this sort of thing again? He will. He can't control himself. He's got to be stopped . . .*"

It all happened so fast that now, looking back, I'm not sure I've got it straight. The bailiff came up behind John and put his arms around his chest. John must have reached back with his right hand and slipped the revolver out of its holster: I don't know because I was on his left side and couldn't see anything except the gun coming up like a huge metal bird. I remember noticing it was a .38 Police Special, and the hammer was falling as it rose. The bailiff fell back in shock, John placed the end of the barrel above his right ear, pointing upwards, everyone gasped, the fingers of his left hand still drummed incongruously at his side. I was looking at them when the explosion came, deafening in the confined space. The fingers shot out straight, trembled rigidly, and then crumpled up like charred paper. John fell to the table, twisted on to his left side, the gun still in his right hand. I could smell burning hair. There was blood all over Cindy's dress, and a patch of John's scalp hung down over his ear. Blood pumped from the wound; underneath I could see white stuff turning red. I'm afraid I don't remember anything more, because at that moment I fainted.

I think it was six weeks later that Cindy and I saw John Norton the next and last time. He was recovering nicely, and took great pride in telling us how he had regained control of the left side of his body. However he still couldn't walk without crutches, and his left hand remained curled up, lifeless as an artificial limb. I spoke first.

"John, you're lucky to be alive. The surgeons said a half inch deflection and you'd never have recovered consciousness."

"That's why I aimed it upwards. So I wouldn't hit *my* brain."

"But John," asked Cindy, "don't you miss Henry at all?"

"No. He got what he deserved. Only thing is . . ."

"Yes?"

"I'm sorry I don't have anyone to play chess with any more."

"Oh?" I felt embarrassed. "Is there anything we can do for you?"

"Yes," he said. "I'm worried."

"About what?"

"I keep waiting for Mr. Carbonari to come and arrest me. But he hasn't come."

"Why should he, John?"

"I killed Henry in front of everyone, didn't I?"

Cindy looked at me and I at her. "You're very logical about this, John," I said, "but you remember what the judge said to the jury. There was no legal person named Henry. The most Carbonari could do is charge you with attempted suicide, and no one has been brought to trial on that charge in this State for years."

He looked puzzled at first, then smiled and shrugged his shoulders. "All this is too complicated for me," he said. "But I'll tell you one thing."

"What's that?"

"If I ever do get into trouble again I'll get you as my lawyer, Mr. Shapman. You and Miss Adams here."

I smiled and put my arm around Cindy. As we stood up to say goodbye Cindy couldn't resist telling him she would soon be Mrs. Shapman, and that we were going into criminal law as Shapman and Shapman.

She was so excited I don't think she noticed I had my hand under her skirt. But *I* did.

Author's Note

There has never to my knowledge been anyone with Marchiafava-Bignami Disease who subsequently developed a sexual aberration and murdered his wife. Thus any resemblance between John Norton and actual persons, living or deceased, is purely fortuitous.

However the occurrence of intermanual conflicts in persons whose cerebral hemispheres have been disconnected by injury or disease of the corpus callosum is well known (see, for example, C. M. Fisher, 1963: "Symmetrical Mirror Movements and Left Ideomotor Apraxia", in *Transactions of the American Neurological Association*, Vol. 88). It is also well known that each hemisphere constitutes a distinct and in some ways functionally independent centre of consciousness (see R. W. Sperry. M. S. Gazzaniga and J. E. Bogen, 1969: "Interhemispheric Relationships: the Neocortical Commissures; Syndromes of Hemisphere Disconnection", in *Handbook of Clinical Neurology*, Vol. IV).

That interhemispheric rivalry would ever take the sustained and dramatic form I have described in this story is doubtful. Nevertheless if anything like this did happen it is certain we are unprepared to deal with it: as Judge Deakin in the story said, we have no legal precedent for recognising two persons in control of a single body. And that may be justification enough for writing about the problem in fictional form.